Pawns

Praise for Brian Gallagher's other books:

Friend or Foe

'Beautiful writing, great character development.' *Voya Magazine*

'An exciting adventure story.' *Irish Examiner*

Stormclouds

'This accurate depiction of violence ... will surprise and educate many. A worthy accomplishment.' *Kirkus Reviews*

Secrets and Shadows

'Heart-stopping action.' *Evening Echo*

'Weav[es] historic fact and period detail into a fictional but nevertheless entirely credible story ... Nail-biting.' *Books Ireland*

Taking Sides

'Gripping right from its first page ... Dramatic action and storytelling skill.' *Evening Echo*

Across the Divide

'The atmosphere of a troubled city awash with tension and poverty is excellently captured.' *Irish Examiner*

Arrivals

'[Brian Gallagher is] one of Ireland's finest authors of historical fiction for any age ... a consummate storyteller.' *gobblefunked.com*

BRIAN GALLAGHER was born in Dublin. He is a full-time writer whose plays and short stories have been produced in Ireland, Britain and Canada. He has worked extensively in radio and television, writing many dramas and documentaries.

Brian is the author of four adult novels, and his other books of historical fiction for young readers are *One Good Turn* and *Friend or Foe* – both set in Dublin in 1916; *Stormclouds*, which takes place in Northern Ireland during the turbulent summer of 1969; *Secrets and Shadows*, a spy novel that begins with the North Strand bombings during the Second World War; *Taking Sides*, about the Irish Civil War; *Across the Divide*, set during the 1913 Lockout, and *Arrivals*, a time-slip novel set between modern and early-twentieth-century Ontario. Brian lives with his family in Dublin.

Pawns

Ireland's War of Independence

One wrong move
could be fatal

Brian Gallagher

THE O'BRIEN PRESS
DUBLIN

First published 2017 by The O'Brien Press Ltd,
12 Terenure Road East, Rathgar, Dublin 6, D06 HD27, Ireland.
Tel: +353 1 4923333; Fax: +353 1 4922777
E-mail: books@obrien.ie
Website: www.obrien.ie
The O'Brien Press is a member of Publishing Ireland.

ISBN: 978-1-84717-893-0

7 6 5 4 3 2 1
20 19 18 17

Printed and bound by CPI Group (UK) Ltd, Croydon, CR0 4YY.

The paper in this book is produced using pulp from managed forests.

Published in:

DUBLIN

UNESCO
City of Literature

DEDICATION

To Deirdre and Vincent – thanks for the many years of friendship

ACKNOWLEDGEMENTS

My sincere thanks to Michael O'Brien for supporting the idea of a novel dealing with the War of Independence and the Sack of Balbriggan, to my editor, Helen Carr, for her excellent advice and editing, to publicists Ruth Heneghan and Geraldine Feehily for all their efforts on my behalf, to Emma Byrne for her superb work on cover design, and to everyone at The O'Brien Press, with whom, as ever, it's a pleasure to work.

My thanks also go to Hugh McCusker for his painstaking proof-reading, and I'm grateful to Denis Courtney for his support, and to Sara Hangan, Emanuelle Landais, Paul Flanagan, and Conor Browne, four young readers who shared with me their views of an early draft of the story.

My sincere thanks go to Fingal Arts Office for their bursary support.

During research in Balbriggan Library I was extended every courtesy and assistance by Assumpta Hickey and Colm Timmons, and my thanks also go to Susan Lovatt of Fingal Libraries and to Liz Eastwood in Balbriggan Chamber of Commerce.

The expertise of all of the above was freely shared with me, but any errors, or opinions expressed, are mine and mine alone.

And finally, no amount of thanks could express my gratitude for the constant support and encouragement of my family, Miriam, Orla and Peter.

PROLOGUE

SEPT 20th 1920

BRIDGE SREET, BALBRIGGAN, NORTH
COUNTY DUBLIN

J ohnny Dunne tried to dampen his fear. Law and order had broken down tonight, and buildings were blazing all over town. What made it a true nightmare was that the people in charge – the police – were the ones setting the fires and running amok.

Johnny's heart pounded and his throat stung from the foul-smelling smoke. He stood uncertainly on the pavement. He wanted to go forward, but was kept back by the heat from a burning public house just across the roadway. The fire roared as it consumed the building, the flames dancing crazily against the dark backdrop of the evening sky.

For the last two years a battle for independence had been fought by the Irish Republican Army with the forces of the British Crown. Earlier in the day two police officers had been killed in Balbriggan, and now policemen in lorries had descended on the town to avenge the death of their colleagues. The nearby base at Gormanston was the headquarters of the dreaded Black and Tans, a mercenary police force sent to Ireland to support the local constabulary. The Black and Tans had a reputation for brutality, and drunken Tans had been known to burn buildings, loot premises, and shoot people without hesitation.

Johnny knew that the smart thing would be to flee the town until the Black and Tans had satisfied their need for vengeance. But who could tell how much of Balbriggan would be left standing by then? And fleeing would mean turning his back on his friends. Johnny didn't see himself as a hero, but he hated the idea of being a coward, and he wouldn't run away.

Besides, if he fled now he wouldn't know whether or not the local band hall had survived the inferno. If it was burnt down it would be a disaster for Johnny. Normally the band members brought their instruments home after rehearsals, but last week he had left his precious clarinet in the storage cupboard. It needed a minor repair, and Mr Tardelli, the band leader, had promised to have it fixed for him.

The clarinet was the only thing of value that Johnny owned, and he couldn't bear to lose it. On turning thirteen last year, he had left St Mary's Orphanage to work in Balbriggan's Mill Hotel. The brother in charge of the orphanage band had allowed him to take the clarinet as a parting gift – one of the few kindnesses Johnny had been shown in the orphanage – and he treasured the instrument.

Each Friday night he made music in the band hall with his friends Alice and Stella, and it was the only time of the week when Johnny felt the equal of everyone else. If he lost the clarinet now it would take years to save for a replacement on his meagre wages. No, he decided, he simply had to get to the band room and retrieve the instrument.

He turned his back on Clonard Street where thatched cottages were blazing fiercely. Their roofs had been doused in petrol by the Tans, and terrified families were abandoning their homes and escaping westwards towards the fields of Clonard, the rise that overlooked the town. Johnny's instinct was to join them, but he forced himself to go in the opposite direction. He started up Bridge Street, raising his hands to shield his face from the heat of the burning buildings. Crossing the road, he was about to turn into George's Hill when his way was suddenly blocked by a Tan. The man pointed a Webley revolver at Johnny's chest.

'Where do you think you're going?' he demanded.

'I'm…I'm trying to get home.' Johnny thought it was a better answer than saying he was trying to salvage a clarinet.

'What the Hell are you doing out at this hour?'

Johnny felt like saying that if the Tans weren't wrecking Balbriggan he'd be asleep in bed. Instead he stayed calm and held the man's gaze.

Always look a questioner in the eye. Mr O'Shea had drilled it into him when training him in spying techniques. *Don't stare someone out of it, but don't drop your gaze. And keep your voice sounding relaxed and confident - like you're totally innocent.*

'I was staying in my friend's house. But houses near his are on fire, so I wanted to go home.'

Johnny wasn't sure if the man believed him. Other Tans might be drunk, but this man seemed sober and alert.

'Why isn't your friend with you?'

'He went to stay with his aunt.'

'But the aunt didn't take you in?'

'I didn't go to the aunt's. I said I'd rather go home.'

The man still had the gun aimed threateningly. Johnny was tempted to try harder to convince him, but he forced himself to follow Mr O'Shea's advice. *Don't blabber when you're being questioned. Don't refuse to answer, but don't seem too eager to please.*

'You came from Clonard Street, didn't you?'

'Yes.'

'Full of Shinners up there,' said the Tan challengingly. 'That's why we torched it. You a little Shinner too?'

If only you knew the half of it! thought Johnny. Instead he shook his head. 'No, I'm not.'

'That's what all the Shinners say – when we're around. Not so cocky then.'

Johnny had been trained by Mr O'Shea to stay as close to the truth as possible. But sometimes a really big lie did the trick, according to Mr O, who had spied for years beneath the noses of the British.

Time for the big lie. 'I'm actually for King and Country,' said Johnny. 'My dad fought in the Great War.'

'Yeah?' The Tan didn't lower the Webley, but he seemed a little less aggressive.

'He served with the Dublin Fusiliers.'

'Where did he serve?'

'Suvla Bay,' Johnny answered, grateful that Mr O'Shea believed in studying the enemy's background as much as possible. 'Fought with the Seventh Battalion 'till a Turkish sniper wounded him.'

Still the man didn't lower the pistol, and Johnny began to fear that his lies might blow up in his face.

'Seventh Battalion?' queried the Tan.

'Yes,' replied Johnny, praying he hadn't made some mistake.

The man held Johnny's gaze for what seemed a long time. Then he nodded and lowered the gun. 'Brave men in the Seventh.'

Johnny felt a surge of relief but was careful not to show it. 'Yes, they were,' he said.

'Not like these Shinner scum.'

'No.'

Johnny was aware that the longer he was kept here the greater the chance of the band hall being destroyed. 'So, is it OK if I head home?'

'Yes. But mind your step. Feelings are running high.'

'Right.'

Johnny nodded briskly in farewell, then ran along George's Hill in the direction of the seafront. The night air was pierced with screams, shouts, and drunken laughter, and flames licked noisily from the roofs and windows of burning buildings. Johnny was about to make a left turn when another Tan stepped unsteadily out of a doorway and into the middle of the road.

'Whoa there, sonny!'

From his slurred speech and unsteady gait Johnny realised that this man had been drinking. *No*, he thought, *he couldn't waste more time being quizzed by a drunk*. Johnny knew that it was risky to ignore an order from a Black and Tan, but he didn't care. 'Sorry mister, but my nan's house is on fire!' he cried. Without breaking stride, Johnny zig-zagged, side-stepping the drunken Tan.

The man shouted angrily, and Johnny prayed that he wouldn't

get a bullet in the back. He crouched low as he ran, to make himself a smaller target, then suddenly he was around the corner. He sprinted in case the Tan might follow him and take a pot shot. No shot was fired though, and Johnny slowed down to catch his breath.

He realised that what he had done was dangerous, but he felt exhilarated at defying the Tan and getting away with it. His satisfaction was short lived, however, and when he turned the next corner he saw that the band hall was also on fire.

Unlike the thatched cottages on Clonard Street it wasn't blazing wildly, and Johnny ran forward again, hoping that it might be possible to rescue his clarinet before the place was destroyed.

He ran round to the rear of the hall. There was nobody in sight, and Johnny swiftly scaled the back wall and dropped down into the small yard. He could feel the heat from the fire, but he didn't hesitate, and made for the back door. He lifted the potted plant under which the spare key was kept. It was hard to see with no lights on in the hall and the only illumination coming from the dancing flames. Johnny felt a stab of panic on not locating the key. He dropped to his knees, pushed the pot away and felt the ground. This time his hand closed on the metal of the back door key, and Johnny quickly rose and inserted it in the door.

He turned the key and was about to swing open the door when he stopped dead. If he opened it would the flames suddenly escape from the building, burning anything in their path? Or was it the other way around? Would air from outside flow into the hall and fan the flames? He didn't know, but either way he couldn't just stay here. Before he might lose his nerve he acted. Standing at arm's length behind the door, he swung it open. To his relief flames didn't erupt outwards, and he stepped inside the hall. He was struck by a wall of heat and wracked by a fit of coughing as smoke from the burning roof hit his lungs. He pulled a handkerchief from his pocket and tied it around his face, then crossed the room towards the cupboard where his clarinet had been left. The fire was spreading rapidly along the rafters, and he would have to get out before the roof caved in. But having come this far, he couldn't go without the instrument.

He pulled open the cupboard, and there was the clarinet in its case, exactly where he had left it. Johnny scooped it up, then turned to cross the room. He was halfway to the door when he heard a loud crack. To his horror the ceiling began to collapse. Burning wooden beams started to fall, and Johnny's stomach tightened with fear.

He made for the door, but a huge wooden beam fell before him in a shower of sparks. Johnny jerked back instinctively, crying out as more masonry from the ceiling fell on top of him. He felt a heavy blow to his head, and sank to the rubble-strewn floor as the rest of the ceiling collapsed into the room.

PART ONE

ASSEMBLY

CHAPTER ONE

BLOOR PRIVATE PSYCHIATRIC CLINIC, TORONTO, CANADA

JANUARY 1919

'How often do you have the nightmares now?'

Stella Radcliffe looked at Dr Colton, who sat facing her in a leather armchair. His consulting rooms were airy, and Stella could see the snow-covered trees in the back garden of the clinic, their branches swaying against a clear blue sky. Despite Toronto being bathed in winter sunshine it was bitterly cold outside. It was always warm and comforting in Dr Colton's rooms, however, and Stella responded to his sympathetic query.

'I'm having them less often,' she said.

'Roughly how frequently?'

'It used to be about once a week. Now it's two weeks since I've had one.'

'That's real progress, Stella.'

'Thank you.'

Dr Colton smiled, and when he did he looked younger than the fifty or so years that Stella had guessed as his age.

'Thank yourself,' he said. 'You've been brave and honest. Key elements in your recovery.'

Stella wasn't sure if that was entirely true, but she smiled back at the psychiatrist all the same. She suspected that lots of doctors would treat an eleven-year-old girl like a child, but Colton didn't talk down to her, and she liked him for it. She had been coming to see him for nine weeks now – she remembered the exact day because it coincided with Armistice Day, when the Great War had ended.

It had been a bittersweet day, with Stella hugely relieved that her English father had survived the war, despite having fought many battles with the Royal Flying Corp, and later the Royal Air Force. But it had been a stressful day too, with her mother bringing her to the Bloor Clinic for the first time, to start treatment with Dr Colton.

'You do understand that what happened in Banff wasn't your fault?' he said now.

Stella knew the answer that he wanted to hear. He had been so understanding and supportive over the nine weeks that she didn't want to disappoint him. And much of the time she agreed with his diagnosis, even if she still tossed and turned some nights over the tragedy in Banff.

'Stella?'

'Yes. I understand that now.'

'Sure?'

'Yes. Really, I do.'

And mostly she did, so it wasn't a lie, she told herself. 'And thank you,' she added, 'for…for everything.'

'That's why I'm here,' said Colton. 'Which brings us neatly to my next point.'

He paused, and Stella looked at him expectantly.

'I think it's time to stop our weekly sessions,' Colton said.

'Really?'

'Yes, I'm very pleased with how you've done.'

'So…how often would we meet?'

'I don't think we need to meet further. This can be our last session.'

Stella didn't know how to reply. She had grown dependent on the soft-spoken doctor who had gently probed her fears and offered guidance.

'Don't worry,' he said. 'If you need care it's available. I've an excellent colleague I can refer you to. Though I genuinely feel you won't need it.'

Stella looked at him in confusion. She was pleased that Colton was so confident for her, but why he was withdrawing as her doctor? 'If I need someone, why can't I see you?' she asked.

Dr Colton's eyes sparkled with humour. 'I've been known to make house calls, but not three thousand miles away.'

'Sorry?'

'No, *I'm* sorry,' said Colton. 'I shouldn't be whimsical. Let me explain.'

'Please.'

'Your father has been offered a promotion to Wing Commander in the air force. It means your family going to Europe.'

'What?! He…he never said.'

'He loves you very much, Stella. He didn't want to put you under pressure. But assuming I feel you can be discharged today… well, then the plan is for all of you to make a new start.'

'Right…'

'And you are well enough. Truly.'

'OK.'

'Though I'll give you a referral letter to a colleague of mine who practises in Dublin. Dr William Moore. If you need care he'll see you.'

'Dublin?'

'Yes,' answered Colton, 'the capital of Ireland. Your father would be commanding officer of an RAF base.'

'And Mom and I would move to Dublin?'

'Just north of Dublin, apparently. A town called Balbriggan.'

'I've…I've never been outside Canada.'

'Why not treat it as a fresh start? A fresh start and an adventure.

What do you think?'

Stella's head was reeling, but she forced herself to nod. 'Yes,' she said. 'That's what it will be then. A fresh start and an adventure...'

CHAPTER TWO

THE MILL HOTEL, BALBRIGGAN

DECEMBER 1919

Alice Goodman looked playfully at her mother. 'Can I ask a question, Mam?'

'Of course.'

Her mother was sitting behind the hotel's reception desk, checking the bar accounts. As the owner of the Mill Hotel she was smartly dressed, as usual, though Alice felt Mam's clothes were a bit old-fashioned for a widow in her forties.

'What do you want to know?' her mother said, putting down the accounts and looking at Alice over the rim of her glasses.

'Why do waiters like guerrillas better than flies?'

'For Goodness sake, Alice!'

'Come on, Mam, it's a hotel joke. We should know stuff like this.'

'I'm the *proprietor*, Alice, not a music hall comic.'

Alice was about to argue, but her mother raised her hands in good-humoured surrender. 'All right then. Why do waiters like guerrillas better than flies?'

''Cause you never hear a customer saying: "Waiter, there's a guerrilla in my soup!"'

Her mother laughed, even as she shook her head. 'Honestly, where do you get them from?'

'From Johnny. He's brilliant at remembering jokes.'

'Is he now? Maybe he should just work as the boots, and forget about being a comedian.'

Alice felt uncomfortable. She knew Mam tended to look down on Johnny, thinking that she had been charitable in hiring a boy from an orphanage. But Johnny had worked hard in the six months since he started at the hotel, and Alice really liked him. At first she hadn't expected that they would be friends. She had rarely mixed before with children from poor backgrounds, but Johnny was out-going, and her own age, and he had a knack for making her laugh. And when he joined the chess club and the town band they had been drawn even closer together.

'He can tell a few jokes and still do his job, Mam,' she said now.

'I don't want him losing the run of himself. He's here to clean boots and help out. I'm not saying he's a bad lad - he's not. But staff who aren't kept in their place can take liberties,

I've seen it happen.'

Alice was about to respond when Flight Lieutenant Ingrams, a young air force officer, entered the hotel excitedly and crossed the lobby towards the lounge bar. The RAF base at Gormanston was a little north of Balbriggan, and many of the pilots frequented the lounge of the Mill Hotel.

'Everything all right, Lieutenant?' asked Mam.

'Just going to tell the chaps the news!'

'What news?' asked Alice.

Ingram halted. 'Assassination attempt on Lord French. The Shinners tried to shoot him at Ashtown.'

'Oh my goodness!' said Mam, her hand going to her mouth.

'Rum business, to be sure,' said Ingram.

Alice was shocked too but she said nothing. She could see how as Lord Lieutenant of Ireland, French would be a spectacular target for the Irish Republican Army. The battle for independence had been going on for almost a year now but this was a big escalation.

'So what happened Lord French?' asked Mam.

'He was ambushed, but escaped uninjured. Several police chaps wounded, couple of the Shinners were shot.'

'Was anyone killed?' asked Alice.

'Possibly one of the Shinners. No one on our side.'

'Thank the Lord for that,' said Mam.

'Quite. If you'll excuse me Mrs G – want to tell the chaps.'

'Of course.'

Ingram made for the lounge, and Mam shook her head sadly.

'Where's it all going to end?'

'Who knows, Mam?'

And that was the problem, thought Alice. For now, the British were still in charge of Ireland, and her mother extended full courtesy to Crown Forces when they socialised at the Mill. But supposing the rebels won their war of independence? Would people hold it against the Goodmans that their hotel had been frequented by police officers and the British military? Or would republicans accept that the hotel was a public premises, and that her mother could hardly refuse entry to officers of the Crown? *Maybe*, thought Alice, but she wished that Mam was less obviously pro-British.

'I'll let you finish the accounts,' she said.

'All right, dear.'

Alice made for the hotel kitchen, her mind racing. Her mother was entitled to her views. There were lots of people like her in Ireland, who were content to remain part of the British Empire. But the republicans had swept the polls at the most recent election, and there was no doubt that most Irish people now wanted either Home Rule from Britain or full independence. Alice was aware that Johnny strongly believed in independence, though she had been careful not to reveal his beliefs to Mam.

Alice was somewhere between her mother and Johnny in her views, but she was looking forward to telling Johnny the news about Lord French and hearing his reaction. She entered the kitchen, where Mrs Nagle, the cook, was preparing vegetables for the dinner.

'Any sign of Johnny?'

Mrs Nagle didn't look up, her stocky right arm a blur as she sliced carrots. 'Out the back,' she answered.

'Thanks.'

Alice continued out into the rear yard, the December air sharp and clear after the warmth of the hotel. Johnny was stacking empty bottles into a wooden crate and he glanced up, then smiled on seeing Alice.

He should smile more often, she thought, *it really changes him*. Then again, growing up in an orphanage probably hadn't given him much to smile about, and being friends with him had made her aware of how sheltered her own life was.

Alice could understand why Johnny's expression was often slightly wary, as though ready, if necessary, to do battle with the world. He was small for a thirteen-year-old, with thick brown hair, a wiry build, and flashing brown eyes that hinted at a sharp intelligence.

'How's it goin'?' he asked.

'Fine. Hear about the Lord Lieutenant?'

'No, what about him?'

'He was ambushed by the IRA at Ashtown.'

'Really?!'

Alice was gratified that her news had Johnny wide-eyed with interest.

He put down the crate of bottles and drew nearer. 'Did they get him?'

'No. People were injured on both sides, but Lord French got away.'

'Pity.'

'Don't let Mam hear you saying that.'

'I wouldn't say it in front of her.'

'Better not say it in front of Stella either.'

Johnny shook his head. 'I wouldn't. You're the only one who knows how I really feel.'

Alice couldn't help but feel pleased. She and her Canadian friend Stella played with Johnny in the town band, and the three of them had also become friendly in the local chess club. But it was flattering that she was the only one with whom Johnny shared his secret republican views.

She could see that he was excited by the news and she put her hand on his arm. 'I know it's all very dramatic, Johnny. But if they'd shot Lord French there'd be holy war.'

'There's holy war anyway. Why should Lord French's life matter more than anyone else's?'

Alice felt a guilty thrill at listening to Johnny's radical views. She would be in trouble if anyone knew she was having this kind of conversation. But the more she got to know Johnny the more fascinated she was by his take on the world.

'Well, maybe his life *shouldn't* matter more,' she answered. 'But he's the Lord Lieutenant, so the people in charge won't see it like that.'

'Too right.'

'And just as a human being, it must be horrible to know that people want to kill you.'

'I suppose so,' said Johnny. 'But he escaped with his life, didn't he?'

'Yes.'

'Not like the men he sent to die in France.'

Alice was aware that Lord French was the General-in-Command at the Battle of Mons during the Great War, when British troops had suffered catastrophic casualties.

'I hadn't thought of it that way,' she conceded. 'Still, there's a high price for taking on the Lord Lieutenant.'

'How do you mean?'

'They think one of the rebels was killed at the ambush.'

'Really? That's terrible.'

Alice could see that her friend was shocked and she spoke softly. 'It *is* terrible. And there's probably more to come. Let's just hope it doesn't come here.'

CHAPTER THREE

THE MILL HOTEL,
BALBRIGGAN

JANUARY 1920

'Hey, Dunne, get me some salt, will you?'

Johnny felt like saying 'Get it yourself, you spoiled brat!' Instead he put down the napkins that he was folding and crossed the dining room of the hotel. He picked up a salt cellar and brought it to the table where Robert Foley was having lunch. Although Robert was just his own age, he was still a customer who couldn't be insulted. Instead Johnny had to content himself with being slow in delivering the salt. He placed it wordlessly on the table in front of the other boy.

'Good man,' said Robert. 'You can go back to the skivvying now.'

'I don't need your permission to do my job.'

'Oh. Touchy, aren't we?'

Johnny realised that the other boy would like him to lose his temper, and he forced himself to say nothing. As the son of Dr Foley, a consultant in the local hospital, Robert was aware of his standing. And in any dispute between a lowly employee and a member of the Foley clan, Johnny knew whom Mrs Goodman would support.

He thought back to the first time he had met the other boy in the town band. Although friendly with Alice and Stella, Robert had seemed to take an instant dislike to him. Johnny suspected that it was mostly based on snobbery, though it probably didn't help that he was a better musician, and was also Robert's equal as a player in the chess club. But it wasn't his fault that he was an orphan, or that he had a lowly job. And why should he be apologetic because he could play the clarinet and was good at chess?

Robert sat back now in his chair. His athletic build and stylish clothes added to his air of confidence, and he looked at Johnny with a slight smirk. 'Cat got your tongue, Dunne?'

'No. Just fussy who I talk to,' retorted Johnny. 'Enjoy your salt.' Before Robert could reply Johnny moved off, crossed the dining room and returned to his work folding napkins.

He could see that Robert was annoyed, and he hoped he hadn't gone too far. Although he wasn't well paid, he treasured his job in the hotel. It wasn't worth risking that to get the better of Robert Foley, especially if it meant being sent back to the orphanage.

Even though he had been working in the Mill for eight months now, he still remembered the joy he felt on leaving the orphanage and its regime of fear. He resented being humiliated by a stuck-up bully like Robert. But anything was better than returning to St Mary's, with its bad food, cold dormitories and frequent, vicious beatings.

Still, Robert would be going back to boarding school this afternoon, so he wouldn't have to see him again for a while. *Provided Robert didn't report him to the owner.* No, Johnny told himself, being such an obvious snitch would make him too unpopular with Alice and Stella. Robert was mean spirited, but he didn't like to present himself in a bad light. *Or so Johnny hoped.*

Just then Mrs Goodman came into the dining room. She exchanged warm greetings with Inspector Basset, a local Royal Irish Constabulary man who was having lunch in a corner of the dining room with Stella's father, Wing Commander Radcliffe, the senior officer of the local air base, RAF Gormanston.

Johnny continued working but watched surreptitiously as Mrs Goodman left the two men and made for Robert's table. He felt nervous but kept his face impassive as he listened to their conversation.

'Hello, Robert,' Mrs Goodman said.

''Afternoon, Mrs Goodman,' he answered politely.

'How are you?'

Johnny swallowed hard. If the other boy was going to report him, this was his chance.

'I could be better,' said Robert.

'Oh?'

There was a slight pause, and Johnny couldn't stop himself from glancing fearfully over in Robert's direction. *No!* he told himself, *don't look nervous, don't catch his eye, just appear to be doing your work.*

'Back to school after the holidays,' said Robert. 'Never my favourite day.'

Johnny breathed a sigh of relief.

'Still, you'd a good break at Christmas,' said Mrs Goodman. 'When are you heading off?'

'Dad's collecting me here after his clinic. He'll drive me to Clongowes.'

'That's nice.'

'Yes, we've loaded my stuff into the Daimler. Though I've just remembered…I left my spare tennis racket behind. Could I possibly borrow Johnny to run up to the house and fetch it? So I can finish my lunch? The maid will get it from my bedroom.'

'Of course,' said Mrs Goodman. 'Johnny!'

'Yes, Mrs Goodman?'

'I need you to run an errand to Dr Foley's house.'

Johnny could see the faint smirk on Robert's face, and he knew Robert was doing this just to treat him as a servant.

Show no resentment, he told himself, *don't give him the satisfaction.* He had heard that the RIC barracks in Carrigtwohill in County Cork had been captured today by the IRA, and he consoled himself that the world in which Robert and Mrs Goodman felt so comfortable was being forcibly changed. And though they didn't know it, he was playing a part in that process. *So let them have their way, his time would come.*

'Leave what you're doing and collect Robert's spare tennis racket, all right?'

'Yes, Mrs Goodman,' said Johnny, then he nodded to her, ignored Robert and made for the door.

'Let's play Tiger Rag!' said Stella, raising her violin to her shoulder.

'I'll try and keep up with you,' said Alice from the piano, 'but it's hard to play that fast.'

Stella knew that there were easier tunes, but it was a wet January night, she needed cheering up, and she hoped that the lively jazz piece would lift her spirits.

'Just do your best,' she urged Alice.

'Yeah, lay down the rhythm and I'll do the fancy bits,' suggested Johnny with a grin.

The three of them were in the private quarters at the rear of the Mill Hotel, where Alice lived with her mother. Mrs Goodman was having tea in the parlour with Stella's parents, while the three friends practised before a glowing fire in the living room, playing pieces that they performed together in the town band.

Stella looked at her friends as they prepared to play. They were an unlikely trio – a penniless orphan, the daughter of a hotel owner, with herself the child of a French-Canadian mother and an English father. They looked different too, with Johnny sporting a mop of thick brown hair, Alice looking typically Irish, with auburn hair and freckles, and Stella herself sallow-skinned and dark-haired.

Having a Catholic mother, Stella had been raised a Catholic and educated by nuns back in Toronto. It was how she had met Alice when she enrolled in the local convent school on arriving in Ireland the previous spring. Although Alice had never been out of Ireland, and Stella had never before left Canada, they had become firm friends, discovering a common love for music and an interest in chess. When Johnny started work in the Mill a couple of months later he had turned out to be an accomplished musician, and all three had become pals through their membership of the band.

Johnny raised his hand now and called out 'One, two, three, four!', imitating the Italian accent of Mr Tardelli, the musical director of the band. Normally Stella would have been amused, but tonight she felt distracted and she concentrated instead on playing the melody. Even so, she knew that she wasn't playing well.

Despite her earlier protests Alice actually got a nice rhythm going on the piano, and Johnny's clarinet rose and fell perfectly in keeping with the jerky tune of Tiger Rag. They finished the piece with a flourish, and Stella lowered her violin.

'Sorry, I went astray a couple of times,' she said.

Alice looked at her. 'Is everything all right?'

'I'm just…I'm a bit worried,' said Stella.

'About your granddad being sick?' asked Johnny.

'Well, yes. But not just about Granddad. I heard Mom and Dad talking. She's thinking of going back to Toronto to nurse him.'

Alice looked surprised. 'Really?'

'Mom has three brothers. But one is in South Africa and the other two are in Quebec and Vancouver. So there's nobody near Granddad.'

'It would be sad being apart from your mam,' said Alice sympathetically.

'Yeah. But what I really dread is that she might bring me back to Canada.'

'I thought your family was settling here?' said Johnny.

'So did I,' answered Stella. 'But now…'

'Well, we'd miss you, of course,' added Johnny. 'But if you had to go back for a while it mightn't be that bad.'

'I really don't want to go back,' Stella said. She had never told either Johnny or Alice the full story of what had happened back in Canada, and now wasn't the time either. The good news, though, was that she hadn't needed to see the Irish psychiatrist whose name Dr Colton had provided, and she only got the nightmares occasionally now. Better to leave some things buried in the past, she decided. 'I like Ireland,' Stella explained. 'I like my friends, I like my school – I don't want to have to start from scratch again in Canada.'

'Yeah, you'd never meet friends as brilliant as me and Alice!' said

Johnny playfully.

'You could still live with your dad while your mam's away,' suggested Alice. 'Or you could stay on in the convent as a boarder.'

'I don't think I could stay with Dad. They're transferring all the planes from Gormanston to RAF Baldonnel – he's really busy.'

Before they could discuss it further the door opened, and Mrs Goodman ushered in Stella's parents. Her mother looked smart in a fashionable woollen suit, and Dad was neatly dressed in civilian clothes. Stella was aware of a hint of drama about the adults, and she suspected that what had gone on in the parlour wasn't a mere social visit.

'Sorry to disturb the rehearsal,' said Mrs Goodman, 'but something's arisen.'

I knew it! thought Stella.

'Johnny, can you leave us, please,' continued Mrs Goodman, 'we need to have a private word.'

'Yes, Mrs Goodman,' said Johnny, rising from his chair and gathering his sheet music.

Stella felt bad for him, hating the way Alice's mother had casually turned him from a friend to a servant. Alice clearly felt uncomfortable too, and Stella liked the way her friend made a point of exchanging a warm farewell with Johnny as he made for the door.

Once Johnny had left, Stella looked expectantly at her mother.

'Dad and I have some news. As you know, Granddad's not well, and needs to be nursed. I'm going to have to sail back to Toronto.'

'Right,' answered Stella, feeling a tightness in her chest.

'The lease on our house ends soon,' explained her father, 'And there's no point renewing it. Mom will be in Canada, and I'll be back and forth between Gormanston and Baldonnel.'

'So...what's going to happen?' asked Stella.

'We don't want to disturb your schooling,' continued her mother. 'Not when you've fitted in so well at the convent.'

So she wasn't going back to Toronto. But being a boarder was still a bit daunting. As if aware of her anxiety, her mother reached out and squeezed her arm.

'I think, honey, that you'll like our solution.'

'Mrs Goodman has kindly agreed to let you stay here,' said her father.

Stella couldn't keep the surprise from her voice. 'Here? In her house?'

'Not quite,' said Mom. 'But in the Mill. You'll have one of the best rooms in the hotel, on the ground floor, with its own bathroom. It's beside Mrs Goodman's own quarters here. So you'll be close to Alice and Mrs Goodman, but you'll each have your own space.'

'Brilliant!' cried Alice. 'We'll be like sisters!'

'OK, honey?' asked her mother.

'Yes. Yes, that's great.'

'And of course I'll see you as much as possible,' said her father. 'All right?'

'It's perfect,' answered Stella, delighted to avoid both the ghosts that awaited her in Canada, and the challenges of becoming a boarder at school. 'Thank you so much, Mrs Goodman.'

'My pleasure, Stella. Sure you're as thick as thieves with Alice – might as well have you both under the one roof!'

Stella smiled, then suddenly felt a twinge of guilt. It was good news for *her*. But Granddad was still an invalid, Mom was going to have to leave behind herself and Dad, and rebellion was growing in Ireland. It seemed selfish to focus just on her own situation. But then again Dr Colton had told her that she couldn't control everything. And he had advised her to concentrate on the feelings that she could control. *So that's what she would do*. And right now her happiness outweighed her worries. She moved to her mother and hugged her.

'Thanks, Mom,' she said. 'I'll really miss you, but thanks for letting me stay.'

CHAPTER FOUR

Johnny walked briskly along the banks of the Bracken river, his excitement mounting. The frost-covered countryside sparkled in the morning sunshine, and the air felt fresh and bracing. In the distance he could see smoke rising from the chimneys of the thatched cottages on Clonard Road, the dark peat smoke slowly ascending into the blue of the January sky.

Johnny had hated winter in St Mary's orphanage, from shivering in a cold bed to washing in the freezing bath house. Now, though, he had a cosy room on the top floor of the Mill Hotel, and he could savour the beauty of the season.

He walked quickly, eager to get to his rendezvous with the commercial traveller, Mr O'Shea. Lots of commercial travellers stayed at the Mill, so it didn't seem suspicious that O'Shea visited regularly while travelling around north county Dublin for a whiskey company. As such it was the perfect cover for O'Shea's other role as an intelligence officer with the Irish Republican Army.

O'Shea was a nattily dressed man with a charming manner, and Johnny remembered the easy way the commercial traveller had first got chatting with him. Looking back, Johnny could see that O'Shea had been carefully testing him to see where his sympathies lay in the struggle between the Crown forces and Irish republicans. Once it became clear that Johnny enthusiastically supported

Irish independence, O'Shea had made his proposal. As a popular drinking venue with officers of the Crown, the Mill Hotel could be a good source of intelligence. Would Johnny keep his eyes and ears open? And report back to O'Shea everything he overheard and saw, when drink had loosened the tongues of RIC men, British officers and RAF pilots?

Johnny had been flattered and excited by the offer and had readily agreed. And now he had slipped out on his morning break to meet the intelligence officer. Johnny felt that they could have had a quiet word in the Mill easily enough, but O'Shea had been adamant that the boots in the hotel shouldn't be seen talking too regularly with one of the guests. Instead, O'Shea had given Johnny a quick nod in the dining room that morning – the signal that they should visit their rendezvous spot, the thick bushes down by the riverbank.

Johnny walked on, drawing near to the meeting point. He looked about with apparent casualness, wanting to ensure that nobody should see him entering the bushes. But the riverbank was deserted and, happy that the coast was clear, Johnny stepped into the undergrowth. He made his way along a narrow trail, then came to a small clearing. O'Shea was already there, smartly dressed in a business suit and smoking a cigarette. O'Shea had instilled into Johnny the need always to have a story ready to explain your behaviour. In the unlikely event of anybody spotting a well-dressed commercial traveller emerging from the bushes, O'Shea would make a point of extinguishing his cigarette – as though he had entered the bushes to avoid being seen smoking during working hours.

Johnny thought that this was taking caution to extremes. O'Shea, however, insisted that with undercover work proper planning could be the difference between life and death.

'Good morning, Johnny,' he said brightly now, taking the cigarette from his mouth.

''Morning, Mr O'Shea.'

'What do you have to report?'

'I heard Inspector Bassett saying he's getting reinforcements.'

'Any idea when?'

'Over the next three or four weeks.'

'Very good, Johnny. Anything else?'

'Commander Radcliffe is planning to have all the aircraft moved from Gormanston to RAF Baldonnel by the end of the month.'

'Really?'

'Yes.' Johnny felt slightly guilty about passing on information that his friend Stella had innocently revealed. But the British forces had huge advantages in manpower, weapons and money, and the rebels had to avail of any advantage that came their way.

'So it won't be an operational airfield by the end of this month?'

'No, but it'll still be a base. They'll keep about forty officers and men on the site.'

'That's really interesting,' said O'Shea, looking thoughtful. 'I wonder what they're planning to use the place for?'

Johnny shrugged. 'I haven't heard.'

'This could be important. I still want to hear all the usual stuff you pick up. But make finding out the plans for Gormanston your priority.'

'OK,' said Johnny, excited that O'Shea was trusting him with an important task.

'You're a good lad, Johnny.'

'Thanks, Mr O'Shea.'

'So don't take needless risks.' O'Shea laid a hand on his shoulder. 'I know you think this is all exciting. But it's not a game.'

'I know.'

'Be sure you do. Things are hotting up. More people are going to be killed. Some of *us* will be killed.

Johnny nodded solemnly. 'I know that too.'

'If you feel at any time you want out…'

'I don't want out.'

O'Shea looked him fully in the eye. 'Sure?'

'Certain. Things need to change here. And I want to change them.'

O'Shea nodded. 'OK, then. Keep doing what you're doing.' He extended his hand. 'God save Ireland.'

Johnny shook his hand. 'God save Ireland!'

Alice liked the slightly spooky feeling of the advancing twilight as she made her way home from a walk along the waterfront. The winter air was cold, but she was wearing her new overcoat that was both smart-looking and warm. Dusk had fallen early, but she enjoyed this time of year and was looking forward to the roast pork that Mrs Nagle always prepared for dinner on Sunday nights.

This evening it would be just herself and Mam eating in their private quarters. But from next week on Stella would be staying in the hotel. Although Alice was used to being an only child, and had friends in school, she loved the idea of a sister – and having her friend living at the Mill would be the next best thing.

She started up the steep hill leading to High Street and thought back to when she had met Stella at school last year. Her first impression had been of a pretty, dark-haired girl with a soft Canadian accent and a slightly shy manner. Some pupils tended to exclude anybody new, but Alice had thought it was interesting to meet someone with a foreign background. And while most of the other girls in Balbriggan's Loreto Convent came from families of at least five or six children, Stella's younger brother had been killed in a tragic accident back in Canada, so Stella too was now an only child. They had also been born within a month of each other and, with music as another common interest, they soon hit it off.

Her friend Robert had also taken to Stella. It had been a relief to Alice, bearing in mind how unpredictable Robert could be. Alice's father and Robert's father, Doctor Foley, had attended Clongowes College together. The two families had stayed close, even after Alice's father had died from a heart attack when she was five, and Alice couldn't recall a time when Robert wasn't part of her life.

He was tall, sporty, and good-looking, and there were benefits to being in his social circle. So it would have been awkward for Alice if he had taken against Stella. And it could easily have happened, under Mam's ABC rule. Alice puffed her way up the steep hill, recalling the first time her mother had explained her theory.

Alice had been seven at the time, and was upset when her best friend took a strong dislike to Alice's favourite cousin, who was visiting. Mam had explained that A and B might be the best of friends. B and C might also be the best of friends. But there's no guarantee that A and C will be friends, or even like each other. Her mother's theory was that everyone would be saved disappointment if people didn't assume that their friends would automatically like one other.

Even so, Alice had been disappointed when Robert took a dislike to Johnny. She had even had words with him before he had gone back to college a couple of days previously. They had been drinking cocoa in the Mill when Robert had made yet another disparaging remark about Johnny, and Alice's patience had suddenly snapped. 'You know something, Robert? You really sound like a snob sometimes.'

'What? Because I don't want to be pals with the boots?'

'I'm not asking you to be pals with him.'

'Then what's the problem?'

'*I'm* friends with him. But still you put him down in front of me. How do you think that makes me feel?'

Robert shrugged. 'How you feel about Johnny Dunne is your business. How *I* feel about him is *my* business.'

'He's never done anything on you.'

'So I'm to be friends with every ragamuffin who hasn't done anything on me?'

'He's not a ragamuffin!'

'No? What is he, exactly?'

'He's unlucky enough to be an orphan. That could have happened me, it could have happened you.'

'Except it didn't. My dad's a surgeon. Your Mam owns a hotel. He's not our class, Alice. You're not doing yourself any favours pretending he is. You're probably not even doing him any favours.'

'So if someone's not our class, we just look down on them?'

'I didn't say that.'

'But you think it.'

'We're not going to agree,' said Robert brusquely. 'Let's talk about something else.'

Looking back now she realised that it had been one of the few occasions when she had challenged Robert. But despite causing an awkwardness, she was glad that she had stood up for Johnny. He was a good friend, even if he had declined to join her on her walk today because he was playing soccer with some boys at Clonard Street.

She turned the corner by the library now, then made towards the main entrance to the Mill. As she crossed the pavement she was jostled by a soldier who stumbled into her path. Even though he had bumped into her, Alice was about to say 'excuse me'. Instead the soldier rounded on her.

'Watch where you're going!' he said, turning unsteadily to glare at her.

Alice could smell alcohol on him and she suspected that he was drunk.

'Leave it, Ernie,' said a second soldier, his speech also drink-slurred.

'Little Miss Perfect,' said the first soldier, looking Alice up and down. 'Think you own the pavement, do you?'

Alice's instinct was to draw back from the man's aggression. But she thought of what Johnny had said about Ireland belonging to the people of Ireland, and she made herself stand her ground. She was tall for her age, and she drew herself up to her full height.

'Actually I do own it,' she said quietly.

'What?!'

'The streets of Balbriggan are owned by the people of Balbriggan. My mother pays rates. So yes, we do partly own the pavement.'

Alice saw the anger flare in the man's eyes. She felt frightened, but forced herself not to retreat.

'Cheeky pup!' said the soldier. 'Think you're smart, do you?!'

Alice swallowed hard, fearful that he might strike her.

'Leave it, Ernie,' said his friend again, forcefully pulling him backwards. 'Not worth being on a charge over nothing.'

'Over nothing? Cheeked me to my face, she did!' He drew nearer to Alice. 'If you were my kid I'd take the strap to you! I'd put manners on you!'

'Well, I'm not your kid – thank God. And the person needing manners is you!'

Before the man could respond Alice turned on her heel and walked away.

'Little Irish brat!' he shouted after her.

Alice didn't look back. Her knees felt shaky, but she was pleased that she hadn't let herself be bullied, and she looked forward to telling Johnny about the encounter. She suspected that Johnny would see it as further evidence of why Ireland needed to be rid of British troops. But Alice reckoned that most of the British officers who drank in the Mill were decent and well-behaved, so things weren't as simple as Johnny made out.

The drunken soldier shouted at her one last time. Now that she was at the door of the hotel Alice turned back to him. She smiled sweetly and gave him a mocking wave. Then stepped quickly through the door and into the safety of the Mill.

CHAPTER FIVE

Stella wished the school orchestra wasn't so old-fashioned. She loved ragtime music and wished they could play that. In fairness, the music teacher, Mr Tardelli, chose modern songs like *After You've Gone* for the town band. But the Year Head of the Loreto Convent, Sister Mary Joseph, had conservative taste, and today Mr Tardelli was teaching the girls a hymn called 'Soul of My Saviour'.

The school's music room felt warm and snug as a January gale lashed at the window pane. Stella knew that she was privileged to be a pupil here, and lucky to be living this past week in a large, comfortable room at the Mill Hotel.

There had been a tearful farewell when her mother had sailed back to Canada, but Mrs Goodman had been welcoming and kind, and it had been fun living at close quarters with Alice. All the more reason not to show her friend up now, she thought. Alice was a moderate musician whose piano playing was adequate, whereas Stella's playing of the violin was much more natural. It was taking Alice a lot of effort to master 'Soul of My Saviour', and Stella found herself deliberately easing off on the speed at which she was learning the piece. Was that ridiculous? she wondered. Or was it only right that friends should be loyal, and that she shouldn't make Alice look bad by mastering the violin part too easily?

When they played with Johnny in the town band he had no qualms about displaying his skill on the clarinet. But that was different, Stella thought. The town band was for fun whereas this was a school class. Her thoughts were interrupted by Mr Tardelli dramatically raising his hands to cover his ears. 'Girls! Please!' he said. 'All I hear is *bump, bump, bump*. Beating out the rhythm. No! The melody must *flow*.' He moved his hands expressively. 'Soul of my Saviour…smooth, yes? Not staccato!'

'Smooth, Stella! *From the heart!*' whispered Alice in a good imitation of Mr Tardelli's Italian accent.

Stella grinned even though she liked Mr Tardelli, and it was hardly his fault that he spoke with an accent. Some of the girls had mocked her Canadian accent when she had started at the school last year, so she was sympathetic to the music teacher as another outsider who had to adapt to Irish ways.

'Shush, Alice, he'll hear you!' she whispered to her friend.

'He won't. He's too busy with Cissy.'

Cissy Murdoch was the least musical girl in the class, and Stella watched as the teacher tried to encourage her. 'You play the right notes, Cissy,' he said. 'But you play like each note is a stranger. No! Each note is a friend to the next one. The notes are linked.'

'Like Mr Tardelli is linked to Miss Riley!' whispered Alice.

This time Stella had to suppress a giggle. Miss Riley was their popular English teacher. Because she was single and pretty there was endless speculation among the girls on whether or not she was seeing Mr Tardelli outside of school hours. Stella thought that

Mr Tardelli was a bit old for Miss Reilly. He must be nearly forty, and his flowing black hair and moustache were flecked with grey. Still, he was handsome, with sallow skin and dark brown eyes. Alice suddenly puckered her lips, as though she were Miss Riley waiting for a kiss, and Stella had to turn her back so that the music teacher wouldn't see her laughing.

She felt a surge of affection for her friend. It was good to have a pal as lively as Alice, especially in the week that was in it. Stella had found it really sad saying goodbye to her mother, and upsetting too that Granddad was ill on the far side of the Atlantic. And the fighting with the Republican rebels was hotting up too, even though Dad, as an air force officer, wasn't directly involved.

Well, there was no point worrying about things outside her control, she decided, recalling the words of Doctor Colton. Instead she winked at Alice, made sure that Mr Tardelli couldn't see her smiling, and went back to practising 'Soul of my Saviour'.

Johnny had been waiting for his opportunity, but he felt scared, now that the moment had come. It was five days since he had discussed Gormanston Camp with Mr O'Shea, and he had failed to discover anything new. Now though, a chance had arisen. Stella was having dinner with her father, Commander Radcliffe, in the dining room of the Mill. She had casually mentioned that she was eating with her father, who was then travelling to RAF Baldonnel, where he would spend the night. Johnny had seen Commander Radcliffe leaving his suitcase in Stella's room for safe-keeping while they dined, and he knew that he had to grasp this chance.

Forcing himself to appear relaxed, he walked past the entrance to the dining room, hoping that the reception desk might not be manned. The room keys were kept on the wall behind reception, and as the Mill Hotel wasn't sufficiently large for reception to be manned at all times, guests requiring attention could ring a bell on the desk.

Johnny's hopes of simply pocketing Stella's room key were dashed when he saw Miss Hopkins, the receptionist and house-keeping supervisor, sitting behind the desk. She was a friendly, middle-aged woman with whom Johnny got on well, and she looked up now as he approached.

'Evening, Johnny.'

''Evening, Miss Hopkins,' he answered, trying to sound casual.

'Everything all right?'

'Fine,' replied Johnny, crossing behind the desk and entering the ante-room where baggage was stored. His pulses were racing, but he knew that the big advantage of being the boots was that he could visit any part of the hotel without arousing suspicion. Miss Hopkins hadn't asked him what his business was in the ante-room, and as soon as he closed the door he made for the top drawer of a press that stood against the wall. He quietly slid the drawer open, then took out the master key that would unlock any guest room in the hotel. The master key was on a large circular ring, and he slipped it into his trousers pocket. He exited past the reception desk, nodding in farewell to Miss Hopkins and striving to keep his pace unhurried-looking.

He turned down the corridor, out of her sight. He continued until he reached the door of Stella's room, then paused. He felt bad about trespassing into his friend's private space. He could still turn back now, and nobody would be any the wiser. But that would be letting down Mr O'Shea, and the cause he believed in. He stood unmoving, torn by conflicting loyalties, then told himself that a war was being fought and he mustn't be weak.

Without further hesitation he took the key from his pocket and inserted it in the lock. The key turned easily. Johnny depressed the handle, opened the door and stepped into the room. It was large and well-appointed, and Stella had obviously tried to make it as homely as possible. There were photos on display of the Radcliffes, some taken in photographic studios, others taken informally on a family holiday in the Canadian Rockies. There was a picture of a younger Stella building a snowman, and a photograph of Stella and her brother who had died, both smiling for the camera in the back garden of a large wooden house.

Johnny felt an unease at trespassing in his friend's bedroom, but he forced it down. Instead he made for Commander Radcliffe's suitcase that was up against the wall, just inside the door.

He hoisted the case and placed it flat on the bed. He hoped that a locked room would seem sufficiently secure to Commander Radcliffe, and that he wouldn't have also locked the suitcase. Only one way to find out, he thought as he reached out to release the clips. He pressed with both his thumbs and was rewarded with a firm click as both clips sprang open. He lifted the lid of the suitcase, carefully noting the layout of clothes so that he could replace everything in its original order. The clothes were neatly packed in layers, but at the side of the case was a buff folder full of papers.

Johnny's heart started to pound as he carefully extracted the folder and placed it on the bed. He opened the folder and leafed through the papers within. As he had hoped, the contents concerned camp business at RAF Gormanston. To his disappointment, however, the paperwork was mostly technical, concerning aviation fuel, deliveries of spare parts and flight training schedules.

Johnny continued to flick through the thick bundle of papers, aware that the longer he remained here the greater the risk he was running. He came across a file marked 'personnel' and he slowed down, despite his anxiety. There were lists of officers and other ranks, with dates for transferring pilots and ground crew from Gormanston to Baldonnel. Johnny was pleased to see that the size of the force staying on in Gormanston was as he had overheard, and already reported to Mr O'Shea.

He continued rummaging, then stopped abruptly on finding a report from Commander Radcliffe to an official in Dublin Castle. Johnny sensed that a communication with the centre of British control in Ireland could be important, and he read the report carefully. Commander Radcliffe stated that the RAF would have transferred to Baldonnel by late January, leaving the camp under a care and maintenance company of officers and airmen. Suddenly Johnny read a sentence that leaped off the page at him. *From February onwards it would be feasible to start preparations for accommodating the new force at Gormanston, and to adjusting the camp to its altered role.*

This would really interest O'Shea, and he pulled a pencil and paper from his pocket and wrote down the sentence, word for word.

He thumbed through the rest of the file, but found nothing else of interest. He continued checking the suitcase, making sure there was no other paperwork. Satisfied that he had found all that there was, he carefully replaced the buff folder. He made sure that everything was repacked in the correct order, then closed the suitcase and clicked the locks shut.

Pleased with his intelligence work, he lifted the suitcase from the bed and smoothed the top quilt. He was about to replace the suitcase against the wall when he heard a sound in the corridor outside. He stopped dead, his heart rate suddenly accelerating.

Don't panic! he told himself, *it's probably just someone passing by.*

Then there was another sound, louder this time and right at the door of the room.

Someone was putting a key into the door lock.

Johnny acted on instinct and quickly moved to replace the suitcase in its original position by the wall. He heard the key turning in the lock, then the door opened and Stella stepped into the room.

'Johnny!' she cried, starting back in fright. 'What…what are you doing?!'

'Sorry, Stella, sorry I…'

'What are you doing in my room?'

'I'm checking everyone's room on this floor. Someone reported the smell of gas, so for safety we have to check each room.'

Johnny had taken O'Shea's advice to always have a back-up story, but looking at Stella's face, he wasn't sure if she accepted the explanation.

'Why didn't you tell me first?'

'I…I didn't want to disturb you and your father. I thought I'd have it checked out and not have to bother you.'

Johnny looked her in the eye, feeling guilty about lying, yet praying she'd believe him.

'I came back to get something to show Dad,' said Stella, her voice still shaky. 'You gave me an awful fright.'

'I'm sorry, Stella. I'm really sorry.'

She held his gaze then gave a wry grin.

'I suppose it's not your fault. Better a fright than being poisoned by gas.'

Johnny felt a surge of relief. 'The good news is there's no leak here,' he said. 'It might be just a problem with a shore, but we have to check the rooms to be safe.'

'Right.'

'OK, well, enjoy the rest of your meal.'

'Thanks, Johnny. See you later.'

He nodded in farewell and left the room, his knees trembling as he walked away down the corridor.

CHAPTER SIX

'Mam, you know Mr O'Shea in room eight?' said Alice inquisitively.

'Yes.'

'What do we actually know about him?'

The weak morning sunlight shone in through the window, and Alice could see the surprise on her mother's face. They were in their living room, and Mam was sipping a cup of tea while Johnny worked at the far side of the room, blacking the grate of the fireplace.

'He's a traveller for Glentoran Whiskey. Why do you ask?'

'I just saw him in the dining room, and he seemed to be…'

'What?'

'Well, ear-wigging.'

'Don't use slang, Alice.'

'Sorry.'

'And who do you think he was listening to?'

'Inspector Bassett was having breakfast with another RIC officer. Mr O'Shea was at the next table and he seemed to be reading the newspaper. But I don't think he was. I think he was listening to their conversation.'

Alice could see that she had her mother's attention, and Johnny had stopped work.

'Well, if he was listening to a private conversation that was poor manners,' said Mam. 'But you can't be sure of that, Alice. And it's not for us to pass judgement on our guests.'

'I just thought it looked a bit…I don't know. *Surreptitious*, is that the right word?'

'It may be the right word. But like I say, it's not for us to spy on our guests.'

'Maybe he was the one doing the spying. I mean, with the IRA attacking RIC stations and all–'

'Really, Alice,' interjected her mother firmly. 'You've got to stop letting your imagination run away with you. He's a highly respectable commercial traveller, and a valuable, regular customer.'

Alice was about to respond, but Johnny interjected.

'Talking about customers, Mrs Goodman – what are hotels in America going to do?'

Alice could see a look of puzzled annoyance on her mother's face. 'What are hotels going to do about what?'

'Did you not hear?' said Johnny. 'They've brought in Prohibition. It'll be illegal for any bar or hotel in America to sell alcohol.'

'It's a ridiculous proposal.'

'Not just a proposal,' said Johnny. 'Mr Byrne says it'll be the law of the land.'

Alice wished that Johnny hadn't raised this new topic, knowing that if she tried to return now to the subject of O'Shea, her mother would say she was being tiresome.

'Well, it's not the law of the land here,' said Mam, 'or you and

Mr Byrne might be out of a job. So finish up the grate, and get to work replacing the bar stock.'

'Yes, Mrs Goodman.'

'And make sure you've all your work done before going to band practice tonight.'

'I will.'

Even though Alice had been slightly irked by Johnny changing the subject, she felt Mam's tone with him didn't have to be so harsh.

'Can't have a proper practice without our star clarinettist,' she said with a smile.

Johnny gave a quick grin in return, then her mother spoke again.

'And, Alice, you need to get moving or you'll be late for school.'

'I'll get my bag and give Stella a shout.'

She turned away and made for her bedroom, still mulling over the earlier conversation. Maybe it was a bit far-fetched to imagine Mr O'Shea as a spy. But the more she thought about it, the more she realised he always had a sort of watchful air about him. Like he was taking everything in. Then again, perhaps that was how he operated as a successful commercial traveller. Either way, from now on she would watch him closely

Stella had Johnny at her mercy. Normally they were evenly

matched as chess players, but tonight she had outmanoeuvred him.

Johnny stared at the board, then looked up and nodded. 'OK. You win. Well played.'

He offered his hand. Stella knew that he was competitive, but he was being gracious in defeat and she admired that. Being careful not to gloat, she reached out and shook hands.

'You'll probably get your revenge next time,' she said.

'I'll *definitely* get my revenge next time!'

They were seated beside a crackling log fire in a corner of the residents' lounge in the Mill, but being a Sunday night in late January the hotel was quiet. Alice and Mrs Goodman were visiting relatives in Dublin, but Stella had politely declined their offer to accompany them.

In the two weeks since Mom had sailed for Canada, Alice had been great company. Stella, though, didn't want the Goodmans to feel she would tag along on everything they did, and with her father on duty at RAF Baldonnel, she had opted to stay in Balbriggan.

'So, how long have you been playing chess?' she asked Johnny.

'About four years now.'

'No wonder you're good.'

'Not good enough tonight. How long have you been playing?'

'A year and a half,' answered Stella.

'Quick learner then.'

Stella knew that Johnny wasn't one to give false compliments so she was pleased at his praise. 'Thanks,' she said. 'My Dad taught me.'

'Is he a good player?'

'Very good – I can never beat him! Who taught you?' As soon as she said it, Stella felt she might have blundered. Although she knew that Johnny was an orphan, he had never discussed his time in the orphanage.

He hesitated briefly. 'I eh…I learnt it in St Mary's. Another boy taught me.'

'Had they a chess club there?'

'No, it wasn't that kind of place.'

Stella didn't want to seem nosy, but Johnny had raised the topic, and she was interested in his past. 'What kind of a place was it?'

He didn't answer at once, gazing instead into the blazing log fire. Stella felt uncomfortable and was about to break the silence when Johnny turned and spoke softly.

'It was an awful place.'

'Really?'

'The food was horrible, it was freezing in winter, they were always beating us…I hated it.'

Stella was taken aback. 'Why were they always beating you?'

Johnny considered for a moment. 'There was no-one to speak up for us. They knew they'd get away with it. So they beat us black and blue.'

Stella was horrified. But the idea of people being nasty because they could be struck a chord. She remembered how mean some of the girls in her class had been back in Toronto, when word got out about how George had died.

'I'm so sorry to hear that, Johnny,' she said.

'It's not your fault.'

'It's still awful.'

'Yeah. But now I'm out. I felt bad for the lads I left behind, though.'

'You'd friends there?'

'Some.'

'Are you still in touch?'

Johnny shook his head. 'I couldn't bear to visit. I'll never go back there.'

'That's really sad – to lose your friends.'

'You have to make new friends. It must have been the same for you, when you left Canada.'

'Well...yes. But I was lucky. I met Alice, and Robert, and you, and all the girls at school. So things have been good for me here.'

Johnny nodded, then looked at her enquiringly. 'And your da. Are you worried about him?'

Stella was surprised by the question. 'Worried in what way?'

'With all the raids, and fighting and all?'

'The rebels are mostly fighting the RIC. Dad's in the air force.'

'The fight could spread, Stella.'

'I don't think the rebels would dare attack Gormanston Camp.'

'I thought he was moving to Baldonnel?'

'They're moving the planes to Baldonnel. But Dad will still command the men who stay in Gormanston.'

'And eh...what's going to happen to Gormanston eventually?'

'I don't know. Dad doesn't talk about stuff like that.'

'Right.'

'Do you…do you really think he's in danger?'

'No-one's completely safe in war. But like you say, he's in the air force. And they're not likely to fight the IRA.'

'I couldn't bear if anything happened to him,' said Stella. 'It's bad enough with Granddad ill and Mom being gone…' To her surprise Stella felt her eyes welling with tears. Apart from when she had said goodbye to her mother, she had managed not to cry, and now she felt silly to be getting tearful.

'Sorry, I just…sorry,' she said, quickly dabbing her eyes with her handkerchief.

'It's OK,' said Johnny. He reached out and briefly squeezed her arm. 'You miss your ma, and your grandda's sick. No need to be sorry.'

Stella was touched. She did miss Mom, but Johnny had neither a mother nor a father, yet he was the one comforting her.

'Thanks, Johnny,' she said.

'You're grand. Fancy a cup of cocoa and one more game?'

'Sure.'

'I'll get the cocoa in the kitchen.'

Stella watched him go, then sat back and stared into the log fire. She wondered what Johnny's circumstances had been that he wound up in an orphanage. Maybe Alice could tell her. She knew that it was unusual for middle-class girls to socialise with a boy like Johnny, but she liked the way Mr Tardelli treated everyone in the band as equals, and she was grateful that the town band and the chess club had brought them together. He didn't have family standing like Robert, or the girls in school, but Stella thought that a good heart was what mattered most. Johnny had just shown that he had that, and she looked forward to getting to know him better.

* * *

Mr Tardelli raised his hand and called for attention. 'All right, boys and girls, break over! But before we rehearse again – tonight's joke.'

Johnny was sitting with Alice and Stella in the bandroom but he turned now to face Mr Tardelli, eager to hear the Italian's weekly joke.

'Why is slippery ice like music?'

Johnny thought a moment. 'Eh…because you can fall flat on your face trying to play music, and on slippery ice?'

Mr Tardelli chuckled. 'Not bad, Johnny. But not the right answer.'

'So what's the answer?' asked Alice.

'Slippery ice is like music. Because if you don't C sharp, you'll B flat!'

Everybody groaned, as they usually did at the Musical Director's jokes.

'Actually, it is kind of clever,' said Stella.

'I've another music joke, Mr T,' said Alice. 'Why did the boy put his head on the keyboard?'

Mr Tardelli looked at her playfully. 'Why did he do such a strange thing, Alice?'

'He wanted to play by ear!'

Everybody laughed. Johnny thought that much as he liked chess, and playing soccer with the boys on Clonard Road, the combination of music and fun made Friday nights at band practice his favourite time.

Lately his life had been incident-filled. Mr O'Shea had praised him for getting the information from Commander Radcliffe's suitcase. He had also been grateful for the tip-off about Alice observing him eavesdropping. The idea of Alice being suspicious had alarmed O'Shea. He had insisted that he would be more careful in future, and that he and Johnny must be even more cautious in their meetings.

Beyond Balbriggan, Johnny was pleased that the struggle for independence was gaining momentum. He had been delighted to hear that county councils in Cork and Limerick had recently pledged allegiance to the Dáil, the alternative parliament set up by the Republicans. And on the military front, the IRA was increasingly taking the fight to the Royal Irish Constabulary, whose isolated barracks in remote regions were hard to defend.

The one downside was that he felt a bit sneaky in deceiving friends like Stella and Alice. And some of the British officers and RIC men who frequented the Mill were pleasant, so that it seemed slightly underhanded to be friendly to their faces while secretly working against them.

But he was involved in a battle for a better Ireland, and spying and intelligence work were a part of all wars. Besides, as Mr O'Shea said, the British had an army, a navy, an air force, and a large, armed police force in the RIC. The Republicans had to use guile if they were going to win, and he knew he couldn't afford the luxury of being too scrupulous.

'Now, the good news!' cried Mr Tardelli, breaking Johnny's reverie. 'We've been accepted for the festival concert in Howth next May. So *bravo, mia caras!*'

Everybody applauded, then Mr Tardelli held up his hand for silence. 'We do two pieces. 'The Thunderer', by Sousa, that we already know. And one new piece, from the home of great music – *Italia!*'

'What's the piece, Mr T?' asked Alice.

'"Funiculi, Funicula".'

'That's a great tune,' said Stella, 'it's really cheerful.'

'For those who don't know, I play it!' cried Mr Tardelli, and he sat at the piano and launched into the jaunty air.

Johnny looked at his friends. All-out war might be coming, and who knew where that would take them all? But he couldn't do anything about it tonight. So he sat back in his chair and hummed along to the catchy tune.

CHAPTER SEVEN

Balbriggan was a shambles. The gale force winds had finally eased off, but Alice was shocked by how much storm damage had been done to the town. The sturdy Mill Hotel had survived with nothing worse than some slates blown off the roof, but people in poorer areas had been badly hit. Walking briskly in the cold night air, Alice and her friends turned the corner into Clonard Street where chimneys, gutters and even walls had been blown down into the street.

'My God,' said Robert, 'it's like the pictures of London after the Zeppelin raids!'

'Lucky no-one was killed,' said Stella.

Alice looked at the devastation. 'I really feel sorry for the people here.'

Johnny nodded. 'Yeah, they'll be freezing till they get the cottages patched up.'

'They're used to being cold,' said Robert.

Alice was surprised by the comment and looked quizzically at him.

'Well, it's not like they had proper heating in the cottages,' explained Robert.

'So that's OK, then?' asked Johnny. 'The wind can howl in, sure they're used to being cold?'

'I didn't say that!'

'So, what are you saying?' asked Stella.

'We're used to well-heated homes,' answered Robert. 'They're not. So they'll cope with this better than we would.'

'Well, either way, let's do what we can to help,' said Alice, anxious to cut short any more friction. Knowing how Robert and Johnny felt about each other, she wouldn't have opted for having them both along as companions. Tonight, though, Robert was home from Clongowes, and he had called to the Mill just as she was leaving with Stella and Johnny. He was about to say something further now, but Alice raised her hand and cut him short. 'Let's just muck in.'

Robert looked slightly irked, then nodded in agreement.

There were lots of townspeople clearing rubble off the street, and Alice and her friends joined them and began to help. Even though serious damage had been caused, Alice couldn't stop herself from feeling a sense of satisfaction. It was awful, of course, that the poorest homes had suffered most. But there was something uplifting about the way the community was rowing in together, with people from all walks of life working to clear the debris.

Why couldn't people be like that all the time? Alice thought. Before she could ponder it any further an old woman approached.

'My dog!' she cried. 'Millie is trapped! Millie is trapped!'

'Where's she trapped?' asked Stella.

'At the back of my cottage. A wall fell down and she's caught under it!'

'Don't worry, missus,' said Johnny. 'We'll get her out for you.'

'You can't be sure of that,' said Robert.

Johnny turned to him impatiently. 'I'm sure if we stand talking about it we won't get her out!'

Alice ignored the bickering boys and spoke to the woman directly. 'You lead us to Millie, and we'll try to free her.'

'The blessings of God on ye,' said the woman and she turned and made her way across the pavement and towards a side entrance at one of the thatched cottages.

'Come on, lads!' said Alice, as she and Stella followed the woman.

They made their way round to a back garden, and Alice could hear a faint whimpering as she drew closer to a large, collapsed stone wall.

'She's under that!' cried the woman. 'God love her, me faithful little companion! I don't know what I'd do without her!'

'Don't worry,' said Alice. 'Whimpering means she's alive.'

They all crouched down on their hunkers, but in the weak moonlight it was hard to be sure what was trapping the dog.

'I think it's this low beam that's the problem,' said Robert. 'If you could all raise that a bit, I could try to crawl in under it.'

'But if we couldn't keep it up then maybe you'd be trapped,' said Stella. 'Should we not wait for the fire brigade?'

Just then the dog gave a piteous whimper.

'Ah, Millie…' said the woman with a sob.

'The fire brigade will be run off their feet tonight,' answered Robert. 'We can't leave the dog in distress. Pull up the beam and

I'll crawl under.'

'Why don't I do the crawling?' said Johnny. 'I'm smaller than you, so it will be easier for me to squeeze through. And you're probably the strongest, so it makes sense for you to hold up the beam.'

Alice thought this was a good idea, but she expected Robert to reject Johnny's suggestion. To her surprise he held Johnny's gaze a moment, then nodded. 'Fair enough.'

Alice was pleased that the boys seemed to have called a temporary truce, and before she could think about it further Johnny had dropped down onto the ground and crawled forward. 'Good girl, Millie!' he said softly, 'Good girl. OK,' he called. 'If you all grab the beam and lift.'

Alice positioned herself on one side of the stone beam with Stella, while the old woman tried to help Robert to lift from the other side.

'OK, on the count of three,' said Robert. 'Ready?'

'Yes!'

'One, two, three!'

Alice pulled with all of her strength, and so did the others.

'Is it high enough, Johnny?' cried Robert.

'No, I need another inch or two!'

Everyone strained harder, then they were rewarded with a cry from Johnny.

'Yeah, hold it there!'

Alice could see Johnny shimmying forward, then she heard the dog crying out.

'Keep it up!' cried Robert and they all strained to hold the beam aloft. There was another shimmying sound beneath them, then Johnny emerged holding the dog.

'She's OK!' he said

'Millie!' cried the woman, as Johnny rolled out and released the animal.

They dropped the stone beam with a thud, then Johnny was on his feet.

'Well done!' said Alice

'Well done all of you!' answered Johnny.

For a moment Alice thought the two boys might shake hands, but they were interrupted by a girl who ran into the garden.

'They're giving out tea and sandwiches outside!' she cried. 'Free tea and sandwiches!'

The old woman approached, the dog wrapped in her arms. 'I'll never forget what ye did for Millie!' she said. 'I'll pray for you every day!'

'Do, missus,' said Johnny lightly, 'we probably need it.'

They made their way out onto Clonard Street again, and Alice saw that her mother and staff from the hotel had pulled up with a hand cart. Under the supervision of Mr Byrne, the barman, they were serving refreshments to the volunteers.

She felt proud that her mother was showing such community spirit, and she left her friends and ran over to her.

'Well done, Mam. This is a lovely thing to do!'

'Thanks, love.' Her mother looked at her and lowered her voice. 'Smart thing to do as well.'

'Yeah?'

'Considering the politics of where we are.'

It took Alice a moment to grasp what her mother meant. Clonard Street was the most republican area of the town – some people even called it Shinner Row. If, somehow, the rebels won the war of Independence it would be no harm to be seen as a good neighbour. Meanwhile Mam would continue to serve Crown forces in the Mill, claiming that she could hardly do otherwise in a licensed hotel.

'Right,' answered Alice. She could understand her mother's reasoning. But it still felt a bit calculating, and as she turned to go back to her friends a little of the good had gone from the evening.

CHAPTER EIGHT

Stella walked happily down Grafton Street, arm in arm with her father. It was a Saturday afternoon and Dublin's premiere shopping street was bustling with well-heeled people. Dad was off duty today and was smartly dressed in a civilian suit, and Stella had worn her best outfit. It was a rare treat to have her father to herself for a full day in the city, and she wanted to savour every minute of it.

The mid-February sunshine was weak and hazy, but there was a hint of spring in the air, and the crowds were good humoured. But hearing the clip-clop of horse-drawn traffic along the street, Stella was reminded that change was afoot. Only last week it had been announced that the police were to get cars in place of horses. And the police would need all the help they could get, she thought, with law and order being increasingly challenged by the IRA. Two days previously four RIC barracks in west Cork had been attacked by the rebels, and now Stella passed a newspaper stand proclaiming the capture of an RIC station today in County Monaghan.

They passed in front of Trinity College and entered Westmoreland Street. Suddenly her father stopped. 'Tea and a sticky bun, I think,' he said, indicating the doorway of Bewley's Café.

'The stickier the better!' answered Stella, dismissing her worries for the moment.

They entered the tea shop and were shown to a table by a friendly, uniformed waitress. After taking their coats and giving them menus, she came back to take their order.

'Right,' said Dad, 'what's the least healthy thing on the menu?'

Stella was amused by the look on the face of the middle-aged waitress. It was fun when Dad was in good spirits, and she could see by the twinkle in his eye that he was in playful mood.

'The least healthy thing, sir?' said the waitress.

'Yes, we're having a treat. So nothing nutritious, please, nothing healthy – something really bad.'

Stella was pleased that the waitress got the joke, for the woman tilted her head to one side as though thinking hard.

'Well, the coffee slices are full of sugar and cream…'

'Excellent. We'll have two coffee slices and a pot of tea, please.'

'Coming right up, sir.'

Her father winked at Stella, and she felt a rush of affection for him. They were planning to go to a variety show, and then have dinner in town before taking the train back to Balbriggan. It was a day she had been looking forward to, and she didn't want to do anything to spoil the mood. But she had been slightly unnerved about her father's safety since the conversation with Johnny a couple of weeks previously. And she mightn't get Dad in a relaxed state like this again for a while. Gathering her nerve, she looked him in the eye. 'Can I ask you something?'

'Of course.'

'You know…you know the way the police barracks are being

attacked?'

'Yes.'

'And how it's getting worse? I was just wondering…well…are you safe?'

Her father reached out and gently squeezed her hand. 'Have you been worrying about this?'

'Well….just a bit.'

'Don't be, love. I'm a hundred times safer than when I was flying missions over France.'

'Yes…but, when you were flying missions you weren't safe at all.'

'No…I suppose not. Bad example. Let's put it like this. I'm based in Gormanston and Baldonnel – and the rebels will never attack those strongholds. They're going for soft targets, isolated RIC barracks.'

'Right.'

'There are plans in hand, Stella, to give the rebels a taste of their own medicine. Can't say more than that. But they might be brought to heel sooner than people expect.'

'And if they're not?'

'Then the army will have to get more involved. But even then it's not the kind of warfare with much call for the RAF. So to answer your question - I'm fine. Probably safer than ninety-nine per cent of those in uniform. All right?'

'All right, Dad.'

'And while we're talking about each other, I have to say you've been top notch since Mom went to Canada. Absolutely top notch.'

'Thanks'

'So, keep your chin up and we'll ride this out. OK?'

'OK.' She felt an urge to hug him, but that wasn't possible in the café so she squeezed his hand instead. She thought that although Mom would be gone for months, and Dad had a job that took up a lot of his time, she was lucky to be their daughter. Some parents might have blamed her when George had been killed, but Mom and Dad had completely supported her. Now she would be supportive in turn. No matter how long Mom was gone she wouldn't complain, and she wouldn't burden Dad again with worries about his safety.

'Right,' he said as the waitress approached, 'here come the coffee slices! Ready to tuck in?'

Stella smiled. 'Ready, willing and able...'

CHAPTER NINE

Johnny tried not to let his frustration show. He was standing in the living room of Mrs Goodman's private quarters while the hotel owner sat in an armchair and looked at him quizzically.

'Why do you need to join the library?' she asked, indicating the application slip that he had given her.

Johnny paused, knowing that a lot hinged on his answer. He needed a guarantor in order to join Balbriggan's Carnegie library, and he was disappointed by his employer's attitude. He worked long hours for modest pay, he was helpful to all guests and staff, and he had never let down Mrs Goodman in the eight months that he had been at the Mill. Yet on being asked the small favour of signing a guarantee, she was reluctant to oblige him.

'I don't *need* to join,' he said. 'But I'd really like to.'

'We've lots of books here. I've given you permission to read them. Surely that's enough for you?'

'I'd just like to be able to get library books as well.'

'What, our collection isn't good enough for you?'

'No, you've great books here. But they've loads more in the library, and I'd like to read their stuff as well.'

'You're not a gentleman of leisure, Johnny, you've a full time job.'

'And I work hard at it.'

'I'm not disputing that. But you have the band, and the chess club, and the books I've given you access to. I don't think you need more leisure.'

'I'd only go there on my time off. It wouldn't affect my job.'

'I'll be the judge of what could affect your job.'

'So you won't let me join?'

'I'm not forbidding you. But I choose not to be a guarantor.'

'That's the same thing. I've no-one else to back me!'

'It's not my fault, Johnny, that you're an orphan.'

'It's not my fault either. I left school at thirteen. How am I to learn more if I don't read?'

'Why do you need to learn more?'

Johnny felt a surge of irritation. 'Why do Alice and Stella go to school?' he asked.

'Sorry?'

'They go to learn. I want to learn too.'

Mrs Goodman shook her head. 'It's not the same thing.'

'Why not?'

'Your situations are completely different.'

'So they get educated, 'cause they've money. But I'm poor, so I'm to be kept stupid?'

'I don't like your tone, Johnny. It's not for you to question me. Or indeed your station in life.'

Johnny knew there would be trouble if he continued to argue, but he couldn't stop himself. 'That's so unfair,' he said.

'The world's not perfect. But I've treated you fairly.'

'Really?'

Johnny could see that Mrs Goodman was taken aback by his response.

'Are you saying I've been unfair to you?' she asked.

If he said any more there would be no going back. But he couldn't retreat now. All the snobbery, every slight where his employer showed that she thought him inferior – all of it rose to the surface. 'You act like you did me a good turn by hiring me,' he said. 'But I've worked for every penny. You think Alice and Stella are better than me, you make it really obvious in front of everyone. You think 'cause I'm from an orphanage that I'm a nobody, that I've no feelings. Well I have feelings, I'm a human being too!'

Mrs Goodman looked like she was too shocked to respond, then just as she was about to speak the door opened and Alice entered.

'Hello!' she cried.

Johnny nodded, but Mrs Goodman said nothing, and Johnny saw Alice's look of confusion. 'What's going on?' she asked.

'We're telling the truth,' answered Johnny, then he turned back to his employer, his emotions still running high. 'You want to know the worst thing? You gave me a look at a better world. The world where you and Alice live. But you won't let me have any of it. Not even a bit. You won't let me come up in the world, no matter what I do! And then you talk about fairness…' Johnny broke off, a quiver in his voice, then before Alice or her mother could respond he turned on his heel and walked swiftly from the room.

He strode along the corridor leading back to the hotel. Ascending the stairs two steps at a time, he made for the top floor and the sanctuary of his attic bedroom. He unlocked the bedroom door, his feelings in turmoil.

He entered the cramped room, sat on the side of the bed and tried to think straight. He had acted impulsively and he realised that it might well cost him his job. But although that was terrifying, another part of him felt exhilarated. He had stood up for himself. Johnny had heard stories of how the union leader Jim Larkin had roused the workers of Ireland to stand up for their rights. And now he had taken a stand too. Mrs Goodman wasn't a bad person, and was never deliberately nasty like some of the brothers had been in the orphanage. But she was snobbish and high handed, and Johnny's frustration at her slights had been building up for months.

So what would he do if he was sacked? Could he be sent back to the orphanage? No! he decided, he wouldn't let that happen. After nine months of freedom he couldn't go back to the horror of St Mary's. If it came to that he would run away. Or maybe he could get another job, now that he had a track record as a hard worker. But if Mrs Goodman sacked him she would hardly give him a reference for another employer.

Perhaps he could find work that didn't require a reference. But who could he approach? He racked his brains, then suddenly had an idea. *Mr O'Shea.* He owed him for all the spying, and he had plenty of business contacts. But Mr O'Shea wasn't due at the hotel for another ten days, and Johnny didn't know his home address. What would happen in the meantime if Mrs Goodman sacked him and told him to move out immediately? He didn't know. But he would cross that bridge when he came to it. And whatever happened, he would somehow survive.

He breathed deeply to calm down. He had heard this morning that the Red Army was winning the revolutionary war in Russia. He consoled himself with the thought that if things could change radically in Russia then maybe the same could happen in Ireland. His musings were suddenly interrupted by a knock on the bedroom door. *If they were chucking him out they weren't wasting any time.*

He rose from the bed and opened the door. To his surprise Alice stood there. 'Can I come in for a second?' she said.

'OK,' he answered, standing aside as she entered his room. She had never been here before, and it was unusual for any of the Goodman family to visit the top floor, where the hotel workers slept.

'Do you want to sit down?' said Johnny indicating the side of the bed.

'No, thanks, I won't stay long. I've a message for you from Mam.'

Johnny thought that Mrs Goodman should do her own dirty work, but there was no point in taking it out on Alice, so he kept his tone neutral. 'What's that?'

'She's changed her mind about the library.'

Johnny was gobsmacked.

'She said you can join.'

Johnny felt a huge sense of relief that his job was safe. He looked enquiringly at Alice. 'Did you…did you persuade her?'

'A bit. But it was mostly what you said. When she thought about it, she felt bad.'

Alice reached out and briefly touched Johnny's hand. 'I'm sorry it came to this. I know Mam can be a bit stuck-up. But she's a good person, really. So…is that OK?'

Johnny looked at his friend, then nodded. 'OK.'

Alice reached into her pocket and took out a slip of paper. 'Here's the application form. She's signed it and all.'

Johnny took the piece of paper. 'Thanks, Alice.'

'Probably the best thing now…is to act like this never happened.'

'Really?'

'You won the day, Johnny, and I'm really glad. But at the same time…I wouldn't rub her nose in it.'

'Fair enough.'

'Right, well, I better go.'

'OK.'

'And Johnny?'

'Yes?'

'Well done. You've got guts!' Alice crossed to the door and left.

Johnny returned to the bed and sat down, thrilled with his victory. It was an enormous relief still to have his job, and he was aware, once more, that life was never predictable.

* * *

'Smart play, Alice,' acknowledged Stella. '"Tactically sound", as Dad would say!'

'Thanks,' answered Alice, pleased to have outplayed her friend in the first round of the chess club's spring championship, one of the major competitions in the club calendar.

They were in a function room in the Mill that the club used for its bigger competitions, and all around them other players were poring over their chess boards. As though making a mockery of it being the spring competition, sleet was running down the windowpanes, but Alice liked the feeling of defeating nature, and enjoyed the cosy warmth of the hotel.

'I thought I had you,' said Stella ruefully, 'when you lost the knight and the castle.'

'I'm like Mr Churchill!' answered Alice.

'Mr Churchill?'

'I had less men, but I made them fight better!'

Winston Churchill, the War Secretary, had recently stated that a smaller, professional army would replace conscription into the British forces.

Stella laughed. 'You're the only girl I know who'd compare herself to Winston Churchill.'

'Lucky Mr Churchill!' answered Alice, then she looked across the room to where Robert and Johnny were playing each other.

Robert was home in Balbriggan for several days because of mid-term break in his school, but Alice was disappointed with his behaviour tonight. She had hoped that the thaw with Johnny after rescuing the dog might continue. Instead, Robert had been his usual cool self with Johnny this evening. And if anything, things between them were in danger of worsening, to go by the scowl on Robert's face.

Alice reckoned that Johnny must have the upper hand, and her instinct was to root for him. Yet for the sake of peace within the group, part of her wanted Robert to win. As soon as she thought it, however, she felt ashamed. Wasn't that the true sign of a bully – that he made other people fearful of what would happen if he didn't get his way?

Alice recognised that Johnny was every bit as competitive as Robert. The difference was that he could handle defeat more graciously. She thought that how you played a game actually told a lot about you. And just as Johnny was competitive but sporting at chess, so too had he handled himself well after the recent row about joining the library.

Johnny had been as scrupulously polite as ever to her mother, neither of them had referred to the incident, and life in the hotel had returned to normal. That's if life could be called normal with clashes between the Irish Republican Army and the Crown forces spreading throughout the country. But looking back on the row itself, Alice reflected on how gutsy Johnny had been. Had things gone differently he could have ended up without a job and back in the orphanage. Yet despite that risk, he had stood up to Mam. Not many people got the better of her mother, but Johnny had been smart enough to appeal to Mam's sense of fairness. Alice admired his bravery, but was glad that he wasn't grown up yet, when the combination of his courage and his views might get him involved with the rebels.

Her thoughts were suddenly disturbed by Stella gently nudging her in the ribs.

'Robert has just had his scalp taken!' whispered Stella, indicating the finished match with Johnny. 'Should we go over?'

'Yeah. Better make them smoke the pipe of peace!' Alice grinned at Stella, wondered again how the four of them had somehow ended up as a group, then started across the room towards the boys.

CHAPTER TEN

I've a bit of news for you,'

'What is it?' Stella asked her father eagerly.

They were driving in Dad's Model T Ford from Gormanston Camp to Balbriggan, the March sunshine bathing the countryside in a warm yellow glow.

'We'll be going back to Canada.'

'What?!'

None of her mother's letters from Toronto had mentioned this, and Stella looked at Dad in shock.

'For a holiday,' he explained. 'I just got confirmation that I can take overdue leave in July.'

Her father took his eyes off the road briefly and looked at her. 'I thought you'd be pleased.'

'I…I am, but…'

'But what?'

'It'll be great to see Mom and Granddad. But Toronto…'

Dad glanced over at her again, his gaze sympathetic now. 'I know, Stella, that it has some bad memories.'

'Yes.'

'But that was then. You're better now.'

'I know. It's just…when I think of Toronto…that was…that was a sad time.'

'Of course it was, darling. For all of us. But we move on with our lives. We have to.'

'I know, Dad...'

'Besides, in time we'll move back to Toronto for good. This is a way to ease back in, temporarily.'

'And...when do you think we'd move back for good?'

'Not for a while yet. The more senior my rank when I return, the better my prospects. First though, we need to see off the rebels here and restore order.'

'Do you really think that will happen, Dad?'

'Of course. Why wouldn't it?'

'Well, a lot of people want independence. I just read that Syria is claiming independence from Turkey. It seems to be happening all over the world.'

'We can't have that here. If we allow rebellion on our doorstep, the whole Empire could fall apart.'

'Right.'

'The Unionists accepted plans for an Ulster Parliament, so there'll be some kind of Home Rule for Ireland. But it stays in the Empire, under the King. We won't be driven out by jumped-up thugs and gunmen.'

The car turned a bend in the road, and almost as if to illustrate her father's point, they were flagged down at a police check point. RIC men carrying rifles were questioning motorists and pedestrians. Dad slowed down, then indicated the armed policemen. 'Like I said, Stella, we're stamping out anarchy.'

An RIC sergeant who was commanding the roadblock recognised Dad's uniform and indicated for them to proceed straight through. The policeman saluted respectfully, and Dad returned his salute, then began to accelerate.

As they drove past, Alice saw the anger on the face of a pedestrian who was being questioned. In the brief moment it took for the car to pass him their eyes met, and she could understand his burning resentment as they were ushered through. She wondered if defeating the IRA would be as straightforward as Dad thought. He moved in military circles and obviously knew about plans to beat the rebels. But Stella was living in the community. She heard what was being said in the schoolyard, at band rehearsals and in the chess club. And she sensed that while some people were horrified by rebel violence, sympathy was growing for the fight for independence. She gazed out the window, lost in her thoughts, until the Ford pulled to a stop outside the Mill Hotel. Stella stayed in her seat a moment, her mind still racing. What would happen to Mrs Goodman if Dad was wrong and the rebels won? Would she pay a price for the Mill being so popular with the police and the military?

But there was no telling the future, and Stella needed to concentrate on the present, as Dr Colton had recommended. 'Bye, Dad,' she said, reaching across and kissing him farewell.

'Bye, darling. Mind yourself.'

She got out of the car and gave her father a cheery wave as he drove off. Yet the look on the face of the man at the checkpoint played on her mind. She turned and made for the entrance to the hotel. But despite resolving to live in the present, she feared what the future might hold.

Johnny crept silently down the stairs. He planted each foot carefully, seeking to avoid the creakier steps as he descended from the staff quarters on the top floor of the Mill Hotel. It being a Sunday night, most of the guests and staff had gone to bed reasonably early. Johnny, however, had forced himself to stay awake. He had waited impatiently until it was one in the morning, then made his move, quietly closing the bedroom door behind him.

The stairs were gloomy, lit by a low-burning gas lamp, but darkness suited Johnny's purpose. Looking out his bedroom window earlier, he had seen a heavy bank of cloud, and he hoped that it would continue to block the moonlight until he returned from his mission.

He moved slowly but steadily now, and reached the bottom of the stairs. If anyone caught him sneaking about he had his answer ready – he was coming down to the hotel kitchen for a glass of water. Treading lightly, Johnny reached the kitchen door and stepped into its dark interior. A street lamp on the road behind the hotel provided enough light for him to make his way to the back door of the kitchen. He stepped out into the yard, his heart racing. If anyone looked out a rear window now he would be spotted.

And if for some reason Mikey Power, the porter, hadn't left his bicycle unlocked in the shed at the side of the yard, Johnny's plan would unravel.

But there was no use in worrying about things outside his control. He gathered himself, then quickly crossed the yard. He stepped into the dark of the shed, gratified to find Mikey's bicycle in its usual spot just inside the door. A quick check revealed that the bicycle was unlocked, and Johnny gave silent thanks, then wheeled it out the door of the shed and across the yard. To his relief all of the rear bedroom windows of the hotel were in darkness, and he swiftly returned to close the shed door.

Returning to the bike, he opened the rear wicket gate to the hotel yard, then eased the bicycle through the gap. He stepped out onto the darkened street, checked that he had the wicket gate key so he could get back in again, then pulled the gate softly shut behind him.

He mounted the bicycle and set off down the road. The saddle was a little high, but he stretched his legs and pedalled hard. It was illegal to break the curfew, so he took a route that skirted the RIC station. He cycled briskly towards the northern outskirts of the town, eager to disappear into the darkness of the countryside.

The streets of Balbriggan were deserted, and he soon left behind the last of the town's lights. The moon was still covered by a heavy bank of cloud, and Johnny could just about make out the road ahead as he cycled into the night. It was a little over three miles to his destination, Gormanston Camp, and this late at night he encountered no traffic. After about twenty minutes he slowed down. In the distance he could see the lights at the entrance gate to the camp. Johnny dismounted, then wheeled the bicycle over to a gate leading into a field. There were bushes along the side of the road, and Johnny hid the bicycle behind them. Then he turned and climbed the gate, being careful to make no noise. He dropped down into the field, crossing the meadow parallel to the boundary fence of the camp. Johnny had reconnoitred the area in daylight, pretending to look for birds' eggs, so that he knew roughly the point in the camp perimeter towards which he was making.

He continued crossing the field, the faint scent of wild garlic hanging in the night air. He was grateful that the weather had been good recently and that the ground was dry and firm underfoot. Suddenly he stopped. A break had occurred in the cloud cover and moonlight shone through. The better visibility would make it easier to find his way – he could see the boundary fence of the camp up ahead – but it would also make it easier to be seen. Although the RAF had mostly moved to Baldonnel they still had a detachment based here in Gormanston. With all of the recent rebel activity there were certain to be sentries guarding the camp, and Johnny knew he had to be even more careful now because of the moonlight.

Crouching as low as he could, he made his way to the fence. He picked a point where a tall dead tree could act as a landmark on the camp side of the boundary, then stood immobile. He listened intently for the sound of a patrolling sentry and strained his eyes to pick up any sign of movement. But nothing seemed to be stirring. Time to act. Up until now he might have been able to concoct a story for being out late at night, if he was caught. Once he broke into the camp, however, there could be no pretending. At best he would be treated as a thief, at worst a spy. And he knew the traditional punishment for spies. The thought made Johnny's stomach flutter. But if he hesitated now he might lose his nerve.

Steeling himself, he took hold of the fence. It was made of wire meshing, interspersed with thick coils of barbed wire that made climbing it out of the question. But Johnny was prepared for this and had raided the maintenance tools back at the hotel. He reached into his jacket pocket and took out a wire cutter. Starting at the bottom, he began to snip the wires. In the still of the night the slight snap of each cut wire seemed to reverberate, but he tried to stay calm. He told himself that a sentry would have to be really close to hear the sound of wire snapping.

He cut enough wire to be able to pull up a portion of the fence, then dropped to the ground and crawled underneath. Once inside the camp he pulled the wire back down so that only the most thorough search by a passing sentry would reveal that the fence had been breached. Johnny slipped the wire cutter back into his pocket, then rose from the ground. Crouching low so that his silhouette wouldn't be seen in the moonlight, he headed for the camp buildings. Most of them were in darkness, but some still had lights on, and the centre of the camp had outside lights that cast a weak yellow glow.

Moving carefully, Johnny drew nearer to the heart of the camp. Now that he was in enemy territory his senses seemed to be heightened, and he stopped dead on hearing a faint noise that sounded like a footfall. Johnny flattened himself against the corner of a long wooden hut. He wasn't sure if it was his nerves playing him up or if perhaps he had heard the sound of a prowling fox. *Or maybe a sentry.* He stayed motionless. Then he saw a shape moving in the moonlight. Johnny swallowed hard as the shape revealed itself to be an armed guard. The man was walking slowly, a rifle on his back as he patrolled the camp.

Johnny felt his knees beginning to knock, and he pushed them together, terrified that the slightest sound might alert the sentry. The man's route was going to take him within yards of Johnny, who hugged the shadows and kept absolutely still. He held his breath as the man drew level. Johnny pressed back against the hut wall, in deep shadows, and his heart felt like it would explode. Then suddenly the man was gone past. Johnny realised that he was still holding his breath, and he exhaled slowly.

He waited a moment to allow the patrolling guard to move well off, then he gingerly peered around the corner of the hut. There was nobody in sight. Time to move on. His goal was to find the administration block of the camp and to try to gain entry to the offices there. With Gormanston being vacated by the RAF it was important to know what the plans were for the camp. If the new force of mercenaries being raised in England to support the RIC was coming here, Mr O'Shea needed to know as much as possible.

Would Gormanston be a training camp? Or a depot from where they would be deployed to trouble spots around the country? Perhaps even their headquarters?

Mr O'Shea knew nothing about Johnny's mission tonight. But if he brought back valuable intelligence O'Shea would be impressed, and would no doubt overlook the risk that Johnny had taken in coming here. First though he had to find the offices where paperwork regarding plans for the camp would be kept. Johnny moved stealthily across the compound, keeping away from the spills of light coming from the lamp standards.

He came to what looked like an important building that lay in darkness. He couldn't make out the sign above the door in the faint light, so he reached into his pocket. He took out a flashlight that he had taken from the Mill's maintenance kit. Johnny thought that the torch was a brilliant invention – no messy fuel like oil or gas, just a couple of electric batteries. But clever as the design was, tonight it could draw attention, so he shielded most of the bulb with his hand, then switched the torch on.

Johnny knew that this was the moment when a patrolling sentry – and there could easily be more than one of them – might spot him. But there wasn't a risk-free way of doing this, so he bit his lip, then carefully pointed the flashlight towards the sign.

Quartermaster's Stores it read. Johnny immediately switched off the light. The quartermaster's stores would contain records of food, drink and other supplies, and might well give an indication of the number of men in the force that was coming here.

But a store that held food and drink would probably be securely locked up each night to prevent theft. And Johnny couldn't risk a noisy break-in.

Better to stick to the original plan and try to find where the Commanding Officer or the administration offices were based. Unlike the stores, an administration building would have little appeal to thieving servicemen, and might easily have unlocked doors or windows.

He moved off again, keeping to the deepest shadows. At the far side of the compound was a building in which all the lights were on, and Johnny reckoned that this must be the guardhouse. He would keep well away from there, he thought, as he moved through the gloom. He saw another single story wooden hut that was in darkness and he made towards it.

Suddenly his foot banged against something in the darkness and Johnny cried out in pain. Worse still there was a loud noise and the sound of metal hitting stone. Johnny looked down in horror and realised that he had kicked over a fire bucket of sand onto the ground. The clatter from the bucket had been really loud, and Johnny felt his mouth go dry with fear. For a moment he was paralysed, then he turned and ran. As he did so a man emerged from the building that Johnny had guessed to be the guardroom.

'You there! Halt!'

Johnny ignored him and sprinted away. The night air was rent by the shrill sound of a whistle being blown. Johnny felt a surge of terror, but part of his brain had registered that the man from the guardhouse wasn't armed.

'Halt there!' roared the man again.

Johnny ignored him and ran flat out. There was another shrill whistle blast, then Johnny quickly changed direction on seeing the sentry from earlier running into the compound.

'Stop or I'll shoot!' he cried.

The words really frightened Johnny. The idea of a bullet tearing through him was horrible. Whereas if he surrendered he wouldn't be shot. But he would be taken prisoner and interrogated, and they might discover the link to Mr O'Shea. He had a split second to decide what to do. It was a dark night, he was a moving target, the sentry was some distance away, and if he zig-zagged he would be harder still to hit. Without slowing he made his mind up, suddenly changing direction, then zig-zagging away from the compound and towards the darkness of the surrounding fields.

A shot rang out, and Johnny heard it thudding into a nearby tree. His chest was heaving but he sprinted as fast as he could, still keeping low and changing direction every few strides. Another shot rang out. The sound was terrifying and Johnny dreaded the thud of the bullet hitting him. But this time it wasn't as close, and Johnny dared to hope that the shooter could no longer see him in the darkness of the fields. The moon had once again gone behind the clouds, which helped, but Johnny knew that soon the camp would be roused and that they might come looking for him with searchlights. He ran on, then stumbled and fell. Cursing the wasted seconds, he quickly rose then ran again.

Despite his fear he tried to think clearly. In the distance he could hear shouts and whistles being blown. But the servicemen didn't know where he had run to in the dark. And the boundary wall was miles long, and they couldn't know where he had breached it. If he could get under the fence and replace it they wouldn't know where he had exited.

He slowed a little, trying to get his bearings, then realised that he was in the meadow that led to the camp perimeter. But where was the dead tree that was his landmark? In the gloom it was hard to distinguish one tree from another. He felt a rising panic, then forced it down. He would go to the boundary fence and travel along it till he came to the dead tree.

His lungs were burning now but he forced himself to keep going, following the line of the boundary. Suddenly he saw the dead tree and his spirits rose. He dropped to the ground, lifted the cut wire and crawled under the fence. Despite the urge to flee he carefully replaced the wire. Then he ran across the field, climbed the gate and retrieved his bicycle. He mounted it at speed, faced towards Balbriggan and cycled off into the night.

PART TWO

COMPLICATIONS

CHAPTER ELEVEN

Alice sang along loudly as Mr Tardelli played 'My Old Man' on the piano. She was in the audience at Balbriggan's town hall, celebrating St Patrick's Day. 'My Old Man' was a recent English music hall tune, and Alice knew it had nothing to do with Ireland. But it had a catchy melody, and she loved singing the song's slightly boisterous refrain about not dilly-dallying on the way. Besides, the play she was attending tonight was more than Irish enough for the feast day of Patrick, Ireland's patron saint.

Mr Tardelli was entertaining the audience during the interval of 'The Insurgent Chief', a drama being staged by Emerald Players from the nearby town of Drogheda. Mam had declined to attend, claiming that it wasn't appropriate to rely on the business of Crown forces, and then attend a play that was nationalistic.

'But we're Irish, Mam,' Alice had argued earlier in their living room. 'You're entitled to go to an Irish play, especially on St Patrick's night.'

'It's not that simple, Alice.'

'Why not? I know the police and the RAF are customers, but what you do in your spare time is your own business.'

'That's not how some would see it.'

'Mam, half of Balbriggan will be in the Town Hall. Dr Foley is letting Robert go. Commander Radcliffe is even letting Stella go.'

'And I'm letting you go.'

'So why won't you come too?'

'Because the right signal needs to be sent.'

Alice looked at her mother in puzzlement.

'Your presence, Alice, shows our family isn't completely anti-nationalist. But not going myself can be taken by other customers to mean I'm loyal to the crown. We've to tread carefully, these are difficult times.'

Alice couldn't argue with that. For the first time ever she had recently witnessed someone openly mocking her mother. It had been a man called Billy Kelly, who was regarded as a layabout, and not someone whose opinion carried much weight. But nevertheless he had boldly called Mam a West Brit, meaning that she was an Irishwoman who aped her British masters. Previously a man like Billy wouldn't have dared to criticise a prominent citizen like Mam. Times were changing, though, and Alice sensed that the war of independence might quickly alter the balance of power within Balbriggan. But Mam had made her decision about attending tonight, so now Alice was sitting with Robert, Stella, and Johnny, during the interval entertainment.

Mr Tardelli went straight from 'My Old Man' to playing 'The Mountains of Mourne'. Alice thought that this was a slightly soppy song and instead of singing along she turned to Robert. 'What do you think of the play?' she asked.

Robert smiled condescendingly. 'Not really my cup of tea. All this "wrap-the-green-flag-round-me" stuff...'

Alice thought that Robert was trying to sound adult and clever and she felt slightly irked. 'Well, if you can't wrap the green flag round you on Saint Patrick's Day, when can you?' she said. Robert didn't have an immediate answer, and before he could think up a response, Alice turned to Stella.

'OK, Stella?'

'Yes, Johnny's just explaining the song to me.'

'The Mountains of Mourne?'

'Yes. How the man in the song thinks they're digging for gold in the streets. But what they're actually at is digging the London underground.'

'Really? Is that what that's about?'

Johnny nodded. 'Yes.'

'All the times I heard that song, I never knew that.'

'You learn something new every day,' said Stella.

'How did you know that, Johnny?' asked Alice.

'We learnt the tune in St Mary's. The brother in charge of the band explained what the song was about.'

'And the policeman who stops the whole street with a wave of his hand – know what that's about?' cut in Robert.

'No, what?'

'The fella in the song thinks the policeman is at the head of the force. But he's just a bobbie on point duty, directing traffic.'

Alice had never realised that either, and though she found it interesting, she also thought it was a bit childish of Robert to feel he had to match Johnny in his knowledge of the song. *Would it ever be possible to get them to be friends?* she wondered. Before she could think about it any further Mr Tardelli finished 'The Mountains of Mourne', and launched into 'The Star of the County Down'.

'Hey, I know this one!' cried Stella.

'Yeah, it's a great tune,' said Alice. She decided that for one night she would forget about politics and the friction between Johnny and Robert. Instead she sat back in her seat and sang along, determined to enjoy the rest of St Patrick's Day.

A magpie burst from a thicket of bushes and flew away screeching as Johnny walked along the banks of the river Bracken. Johnny started and hoped that the single magpie wasn't a bad omen. He wasn't normally superstitious, but he felt uneasy this morning as he made his way to a secret rendezvous with Mr O'Shea.

It would be his first meeting with the spymaster since his unsuccessful break-in to Gormanston Camp. Johnny had decided not to tell O'Shea anything about that night. It would have been different if he had gained useful intelligence. Instead he had come away empty-handed and nearly been shot – better that O'Shea knew nothing about that.

Besides, there were bigger things to worry about. In the week since St Patrick's Day the republican movement had been dealt a bad blow with the assassination of the Lord Mayor of Cork, Tomás Mac Curtain. As well as being mayor, Mac Curtain was a senior officer in the IRA, and Johnny had realised the war was becoming more ruthless when Mac Curtain was shot dead in front of his wife and child.

Johnny entered the bushes now, the March air cold and damp, and made his way along the trail leading to the clearing that was the rendezvous point. Mr O'Shea was already there and he raised a hand in greeting. As usual the commercial traveller was nattily dressed, but this morning Johnny thought he looked a bit subdued.

''Morning, Mr O.'

''Morning, Johnny. Anything for me?'

'Yes. I overheard two RIC officers talking in the lounge.'

'And?'

'The special constables they're hiring in England to back the RIC? They're coming this week.'

'We knew that already,' said O'Shea. 'Hundreds of them are on their way. Could be in Ireland as early as tomorrow.'

'But they're not coming to Gormanston,' said Johnny.

'Really?'

'Not at first anyway. I overheard them saying the recruits will be put up in Dublin. In the Police Depot in the Phoenix Park.'

'That's interesting.'

'But they think Gormanston will be one of their bases in time.'

'Any idea when?'

'No, they didn't say. But eh…they seemed to think these men will be really tough.'

O'Shea nodded. 'They're hiring ex-soldiers who were battle

hardened in the Great War. They'll be used to brutality. Things are going to get nasty.'

'Aren't they nasty already?' asked Johnny. 'I mean, Tomás Mac Curtain, shot dead right in front of his family?'

'They'll pay for that,' said O'Shea grimly.

'Who'll pay?'

'The RIC. We know it was them. The men who murdered Mac Curtain blackened their faces, but they were seen going into the police barracks.'

'Really?'

'Yeah.'

'And the way things are going, Johnny…' O'Shea looked a little troubled as he seemed to try to find the right words.

'What?'

'You've picked up useful intelligence, and I'm really grateful.'

'I'm proud to play my part.'

'I know you are, Johnny. But…I feel a bit uneasy.'

'About what?'

'About using a boy as young as you. I know I'm the one who asked you to work for us. But things have changed since then. And it's likely to get worse. Far worse.'

'What are you saying? You don't want me anymore?'

'Not that I don't want you, Johnny. But there'd be no shame in you standing down. You've done your bit. And what you're doing is getting more dangerous.'

'I don't care!'

'You should care. You have your whole life in front of you.'

'What kind of a life will that be, if we don't change things?'

'Look, I know the orphanage must have been tough, and you want a better world, but–'

'You don't know the half of it! You haven't a clue what it was like in that place.'

'Johnny…'

'It was a nightmare! And now I'm out of it, and I've a chance to do something that makes a difference, and you want to take that away from me!'

'I don't, Johnny. It would help the movement to keep getting your reports–'

'Then let me do that! I know things are hotting up, I'm not stupid. So I'll be really, really careful. But they don't suspect me. To them I'm just a kid. Please, let me do this.'

O'Shea said nothing, and Johnny could see that he was torn.

'Please, Mr O. This is the first time in my life I've done something that really matters. Let me keep doin' it.'

Johnny sensed that he was swaying O'Shea and he went for broke. '*You'll* get valuable information, *I'll* know that I count for something. Please, let me play my part.'

O'Shea said nothing for a moment, then nodded.

'All right. But you truly need to watch your step. People think the war is bad now – it's nothing compared to what's coming.'

'I understand. I'll be dead careful.'

'OK, then.'

'Thanks. And Mr O?'

'Yes?'

'I won't let you down. I promise, you won't regret this.'

CHAPTER TWELVE

Stella's roast lamb smelt wonderful and tasted delicious, but she couldn't enjoy it fully. It was Easter Sunday, and she was having lunch with her father, Alice and Mrs Goodman, and Robert and Dr Foley. The dining room of the Mill was crowded, but the serving staff were highly attentive to Mrs Goodman and her guests. Stella, however, couldn't help but feel uneasy. Instead of celebrating Easter by eating with his friends, Johnny had been instructed to help in the hotel kitchen.

Stella understood that Johnny was an employee, and that the hotel was busy today. But she still thought that Mrs Goodman could have let him off for an hour, knowing that Johnny had become good friends with herself and Alice.

She hadn't dared to say anything to Mrs Goodman, and had also resisted the temptation of mentioning it to Alice. Before going to Canada, Mam had told her not to intrude into hotel business, and Stella had obeyed her. But still, it didn't feel right for herself, Alice and Robert to be eating fancy food while Johnny slaved in the kitchen. She had never had a friend before who worked for a living, and it struck her just how sheltered she and Alice were. They had loving parents who always looked out for them, while Johnny had no family and had to take care of himself.

Dr Foley was now describing advances in his field of surgery,

111

and while the others listened politely Stella allowed her mind to drift. Looking at the well-dressed customers who filled the Mill's dining room, she wondered how the people here could behave as though everything was normal.

Instead, the past ten days had seen an alarming increase in violence, with a swift backlash after the killing of the republican, Tomás Mac Curtain. A judge called Alan Bell had been dragged from a tram in Dublin and shot dead, a policeman had been killed in Kilkenny, and two civilians had been fatally shot during rioting in Limerick.

The IRA had also burned hundreds of rural police stations that the RIC had had to abandon. But Dad claimed that the tide was about to turn with the arrival last week of eight hundred special constables from England. Unlike most RIC men, the members of this new force – nicknamed Black and Tans because of their uniforms – were battle hardened ex-soldiers.

Stella didn't find this reassuring. It seemed to her that each time one side struck a blow, the other side grew more violent in response. And although the Royal Air Force had limited involvement in combating the guerrilla warfare, Dad was still in uniform, and therefore a possible target.

The conversation had now shifted from surgery to rugby and Stella sensed that Robert was trying to impress his father as he enthused about training with the Clongowes team. Stella found Dr Foley a bit domineering, and she thought it interesting that the normally confident Robert was much less secure in his father's company, and seemed to be trying hard to impress him. Her own father had also played rugby and was listening with interest, and Stella had to keep a straight face when Alice caught her glance and threw her eyes up to heaven.

Stella winked at her friend, then went back to eating her lamb. But her appetite for celebrating Easter was dulled by the events of the last few weeks. And she thought that however much the diners in the Mill tried to shut out reality, trouble was spreading through Ireland – and sooner or later it would reach Balbriggan.

CHAPTER THIRTEEN

Alice swallowed hard and tried to get up her nerve. She was standing in the first-floor corridor of the Mill Hotel. If she was going to break the law, now was her chance. With school being closed for Easter holidays, Stella was visiting Dublin with Commander Radcliffe. Alice's mother had gone to a meeting with their vegetable supplier, and Johnny and the rest of the hotel staff were busy clearing up after the guests' breakfast.

Alice gripped the master key that she had taken from the office, her palms clammy as she tried to control her fear. She knew that if she trespassed into someone's room she would be crossing a major boundary. And if she were caught snooping she would be in huge trouble with Mam. She might even be arrested.

She stood immobile, knowing that this was foolish. The chamber maids who cleaned the rooms didn't start in this part of the hotel, but even so, if anyone else found her loitering in the corridor it would look suspicious. *Come on!* she told herself. *You've started this, so see it through.*

She moved swiftly down the corridor, then stopped at the door to Mr O'Shea's room. Mam had dismissed it when Alice had told her about O'Shea eavesdropping on the RIC officers. But Alice hadn't been able to shake off the feeling that the commercial traveller was up to something. And with the guerrilla war between the rebels and the RIC hotting up, it was important to know if O'Shea had actually been spying.

Alice had seen him leaving the hotel this morning with his case of whiskey samples, which meant that if he followed his normal routine he wouldn't be back to his room until late in the afternoon. *If he followed his normal routine.* Before her nerve failed her, Alice slipped the master key into the lock and turned it. She knew that if a guest came out of any one of the other rooms now she would be caught red handed. Nobody appeared, however, and Alice quickly entered the bedroom and closed the door behind her. The room hadn't been made up yet, but O'Shea was clearly a tidy man and had pulled the bedclothes up on the bed. Even so, there was an intimacy about being in his unmade room – she could smell a faint trace of his cologne in the air – and Alice felt uncomfortable about invading his privacy.

She hesitated halfway across the room, telling herself that she could walk away now and no-one would be any the wiser. *What did she even think she was going to find?* But if she got cold feet now, she would hate herself later. Forcing back her fear, she looked appraisingly around the room. She went to the bedside locker, but all she found there was a detective novel, keys on a keyring and some loose change. There was a table and chair at the window, with paperwork stacked in files on the table. Alice crossed to the window, standing far enough back not to be visible from the street outside. She began to examine the paperwork, carefully replacing each item exactly where she had found it. To her disappointment all of the files related to O'Shea's work for Glentoran Whiskey.

Well, what did she expect? If he was a spy he was hardly going to leave sensitive information on view in his room. If he had any kind of notes on the police or the army he would keep them hidden away, or on his person. Then again, with roadblocks and spot checks being mounted by the authorities, perhaps he wouldn't risk carrying such information on him as he went about his work. So if there was anything incriminating he would probably hide it here in the room. *But where?*

One obvious place was underneath the mattress. Alice quickly checked it out, but found nothing. She looked underneath the bed and on top of the wardrobe, but again found nothing.

Opening the wardrobe, she went through the pockets of a spare suit and pressed white shirts, again to no avail. *Was this a wild goose chase?* Maybe O'Shea wasn't a spy. Maybe he was just a nosy commercial traveller who couldn't resist eavesdropping on other people's conversations. *And yet.* There had been something…something *furtive* about his behaviour when he hadn't known that Alice was watching him.

She opened a drawer inside the wardrobe and found socks, vests, and handkerchiefs, all neatly stored. She opened a second drawer that contained clean underwear and she hesitated. She felt deeply uncomfortable at invading O'Shea's privacy to this extent, but she forced herself to press on. She pulled out the drawer, then ran her hand through the folded white underwear. She searched gingerly, being careful to leave the underwear lying in the drawer exactly as she had found it. Suddenly she stopped, her fingers touching something solid.

Reaching in carefully, Alice lifted out a moleskin notebook. Whatever was in the concealed notebook was obviously something that O'Shea didn't want anyone to see. It could, of course, be love poems that he had written for his girlfriend, or a private diary. *Or it could be the notes of a spy.*

Alice paused a moment, almost afraid of what the contents might be. Then she bit her lip and opened the cover. The entries in the notebook were written in neat, block letters. Most of O'Shea's observations weren't written in full sentences, but in a sort of shorthand. Even so, the purpose of the notebook was obvious to Alice. It was a record of RIC and British Army details. Estimated strengths of units, names of commanding officers, information on transport, supplies and armaments.

He was a spy, no doubt about it.

Alice felt a sense of exultation that she had been right after all. But no sooner had she congratulated herself than she read something that stopped her dead. Flicking through another section of the book she saw a series of dated entries under the heading Johnny D. Alice read on with mounting horror. It was too much of a coincidence to think that O'Shea met someone else called Johnny D whenever he stayed at the Mill. *It had to be her friend, Johnny Dunne.*

What had Johnny got himself into? Although on reflection, maybe it shouldn't have been such a surprise. Johnny had been pretty open with her about his republican views. But it was one thing wanting Irish freedom, another thing entirely to be involved in spying during a guerrilla war. Spies could be executed in wartime, and even if Johnny was too young to be hanged, he could serve a long sentence in one of the awful reformatories that Alice had heard about.

If Alice reported O'Shea to the police Johnny could end up in serious trouble. But if she did nothing O'Shea might draw Johnny further into a violent conflict – a conflict that had become even more dangerous since the arrival of the so-called Black and Tans. Supposing she tore out the pages that related to Johnny and posted the rest of the book anonymously to the police? But then there would be no way for the police to prove that the book belonged to O'Shea.

No, she would need to be cleverer than that. She had to find out more about what O'Shea was doing, and an idea suddenly struck her. The keys that she had seen at the bedside locker were presumably the keys to the commercial traveller's home. If she found out his address from the hotel register she could search his house. There might well be arms or explosives there. And then what?

Supposing she waited until the next time O'Shea was in the Mill to steal the notebook with the references to Johnny? Then she could tip off the authorities anonymously about any contraband at O'Shea's house and have him arrested. Or she could approach O'Shea and offer to say nothing to the police – provided he promised to stop putting Johnny at risk.

First though she had to find out where he lived, and see if there were weapons stored there. But if she took the keys O'Shea would know that someone had been in his room. *Unless she had copies made.* The Mill had a standing arrangement with Mr Regan, the local locksmith. No questions would be asked if Alice approached him to cut a set of keys.

She stood there a moment trying to think clearly. If she went ahead she would be entering a world of deception and violence. And once in that world there might be no way back out. But if she did nothing Johnny could end up getting hurt, or even killed. There was also the risk of a dangerous backlash against Mam and the Mill Hotel if the authorities found out that an employee there was a spy. So far Mam had maintained good relations with the Crown forces, but that could change in an instant if the Tans found out about Johnny. She had to act – there was no choice.

Her mind suddenly made up, she replaced the book carefully beneath the underwear. She closed the drawer and the wardrobe and crossed the room. She stood at the bedside locker and looked at the keys. Then she reached out, slipped them into her pocket and made for the door.

Johnny lost himself in the music as he played 'I'm Forever Blowing Bubbles' on his clarinet. It was a hit tune from a year or so ago, and Johnny was experimenting with it, deliberately altering the tempo and improvising around the melody. Jazz was the latest musical craze, and Johnny liked the way it freed him to put his own stamp on a tune.

It was a mild spring evening, and Johnny had made for the Martello tower at the Back Strand as soon as he had finished work. He was seated now at the rocks below the tower, the sea lapping gently near his feet as he coaxed a lilting riff from the clarinet.

Since Mrs Goodman had sponsored him to join the library he had been a regular visitor. He was eagerly working his way through the adventure stories of R.M. Ballantyne, but also reading every book he could find about music. If he learnt enough, and became a more accomplished musician, then maybe one day he could play for a living. It was just a dream for now – and one he hadn't shared with anyone – but it was something to aim for.

He reached the end of the tune and shifted smoothly into Jerome Kern's classic 'They Didn't Believe Me', one of his favourite pieces. Suddenly his eye was caught by movement down at the beach. The tide was in, but walking along the shoreline towards him were Robert Foley and two other smartly dressed boys.

Johnny recognised them as Quinn and Lenihan, friends of Robert's from his school rugby team, who were visiting the Foley home during the Easter holidays. They had been in the Mill with Robert for lunch the previous day, and Johnny had taken a dislike to them, with their cocky demeanour, raucous laughter, and general air of superiority.

Johnny felt uncomfortable as they drew nearer. Although he couldn't hear what they were saying, Robert had pointed in his direction, and they were laughing among themselves. Johnny turned slightly away as he played, hoping that they would simply pass by.

'What have we got here – is it the Pied Piper?' asked Lenihan.

He was a tall, well-built boy with oiled black hair. Quinn was squat and bull-necked, but had a surprisingly high-pitched laugh, which he gave now.

'Good question, Lenny,' he said, 'good question!'

Johnny didn't respond to the jibe and kept playing.

'I think your little pal is ignoring us, Foley,' said Lenihan.

From the corner of his eye Johnny could see Robert drawing nearer.

'Hey, Dunne!' called Robert. 'Don't turn your back on your betters.'

Johnny felt angry, but he sensed that the best way to retaliate was to keep playing as though the other boys weren't there. He was rewarded by seeing Robert irritatedly walking around to face him.

'Something wrong with your ears, Dunne?!'

The other two boys had now stepped around to face him also, and Johnny realised that to keep on ignoring them might be a bad move. Nevertheless he brought the tune to an unrushed end, then answered Robert. 'Nothing wrong with my ears. But you're not my betters.'

'Pretty cheeky for a boots, aren't you?' said Lenihan.

'I think maybe you're confused,' said Johnny.

'How's that?'

'We're not in the hotel. I'm only the boots when I'm in the Mill. Out here I don't answer to you.'

'Out here you're on your own,' said Quinn. 'And there's three of us. Don't make us put manners on you.'

'Manners? I was playing music and minding my own business. You're the ones started making comments.'

Lenihan drew a little closer and looked Johnny in the eye. 'For a little guttersnipe, you've a lot to say for yourself.' He turned to Robert. 'Is he always this mouthy?'

Robert nodded. 'Yeah, pretty much.'

'Five minutes at the back of the rugger pitches would sort that out,' said Quinn.

Lenihan raised an eyebrow as though amused. 'Five minutes? I'd say more like one minute!'

Robert smirked and Quinn gave his high-pitched laugh again, but Johnny kept his face a mask.

'Cat got your tongue, Dunne?' said Robert.

'Tell you what, boots,' said Lenihan. 'Maybe we'll let you off with a warning. Play a little tune, and if we like it we might call it quits.' Lenihan looked at his two friends. 'Anyone got any requests?' He turned back to Johnny again. 'I take it you do requests?'

Johnny felt his anger growing. He knew that this had nothing to do with music, and that Lenihan just wanted to humiliate him.

'Yeah, I do requests all right,' he said, rising to his feet. 'And I have one for you. Why don't you push off back to Balbriggan and mind your own business.'

Johnny saw the glint of anger in Lenihan's eyes and he readied himself in case Lenihan threw a punch. He knew that outnumbered three to one by bigger boys he didn't stand much chance. But he had learnt in the orphanage that it was better to take a beating while standing up for yourself than to allow a bully to do anything he pleased.

Lenihan, however, surprised him by taking a different tack. 'I think maybe I know why he doesn't want to play,' he said.

'Why's that?' asked Robert.

'I think maybe that clarinet is stolen. You wouldn't buy many instruments with what a boots earns, would you?'

'Might buy a Jew's Harp, Lenny!' said Quinn.

'But probably not a clarinet. So as a law-abiding citizen, I have to reclaim it!'

Moving at speed, Lenihan grabbed the stem of the clarinet and whisked it out of Johnny's hand. He backed away smilingly, and when Johnny ran at him he quickly threw the clarinet to Robert.

'Lenihan' passes to the outhalf!' he cried. Johnny changed direction and moved fast, closing in on Robert.

'Foley passes inside to the prop!' cried Lenihan as Robert accurately threw the clarinet to Quinn.

Once again Johnny switched direction and bore down on the stocky boy. But Quinn was obviously an experienced rugby player and he got away a pass back to Robert. Infuriated, Johnny grappled with him, driving him backwards. Quinn obviously hadn't expected Johnny to take him on, and Johnny saw a flash of shock in the other boy's eyes. Johnny crashed into his ribs, and Quinn cried out in pain. Before Johnny could press his advantage, however, Lehihan grabbed him from behind and swung him violently around. Johnny raised his fists to defend himself, but Lenihan had taken him by surprise and landed a numbing blow to Johnny's solar plexus.

Johnny doubled up in agony and dropped to the ground, the air knocked out of his lungs

'Teach him a lesson, Foley!' cried Lenihan, pointing to the clarinet. 'Chuck it in the sea!'

'No!' cried Johnny, but being winded all that came out was a strangulated cry.

He saw Robert hesitating. Despite the friction between them, Johnny hoped that the other boy would have more decency than to do such a horrible thing.

'Go on, Fols!' said an angry Quinn.

Johnny tried to get to his feet but he had been badly winded and all he could do was look pleadingly in Robert's direction.

'Come on, Foley!' cried Lenihan.

Johnny could see Robert's hand tightening on the clarinet. He prayed that Robert would pull back from the brink and throw the instrument onto the sand at the base of the rocks.

'Don't go soft on us, Fols!' shouted Quinn.

Gasping for air, Johnny watched as Robert reacted to Quinn's exhortation. Chucking the clarinet in a high arc, Robert threw it into the water.

'No!' screamed Johnny. 'No!'

He heard the other boys cheering Robert's actions, then the three of them walked off towards the town.

Clasping his stomach, Johnny struggled to his feet and looked despairingly at the sea. There was no sign of the clarinet, and he slowly sank back to his knees, trying hard to hold back his tears.

Stella strode through Balbriggan, her face grim. Dusk had fallen, with the first twinkling stars appearing in a clear night sky, but Stella wasn't in the mood to savour the warm spring air. She passed St Peter and Paul's church as she strode along Dublin Street. Normally she would have blessed herself, as Mom had taught her to do when passing a church, but tonight her mind was elsewhere.

She couldn't remember the last time she had felt so furious. And she didn't know what she was going to do when she reached her destination – but she had to do something. She walked on briskly, anxious to bring matters to a head while still fuelled by her anger.

She turned into the driveway of a large, detached house, her pulses starting to race as she made for the hall door. The air was scented with night stock, and she took a deep breath, then reached for the knocker and gave three firm knocks. After a moment she heard the sound of approaching footsteps.

The door swung open, and Robert stood before her. 'Stella,' he said. 'Pleasant surprise.'

He smiled confidently, and something in Stella snapped. Before she knew what she was doing she slapped him in the face.

Robert drew back in shock. 'What…what was that for?!'

'You think you're so smart, Robert. Figure it out!'

Clearly shaken, Robert raised his hand to his reddened cheek, but before he could respond Stella turned on her heel and walked swiftly back down the drive.

She half expected Robert to shout or come running after her. To her relief he did neither, and she reached the end of the drive-way and regained the road.

Walking swiftly back towards the Mill, Stella's emotions were in turmoil. She still felt angry, and surprised at herself for acting violently, but mostly she felt a sense of release. In her whole life she had never hit anyone before. And she knew that violence rarely solved problems. But just this once it felt right. Robert had looked so pleased with himself – despite the awful thing he had done to Johnny – that he needed a short, sharp shock.

The fact that Johnny had managed to retrieve the clarinet from the water changed nothing as far as Stella was concerned. For Robert to throw Johnny's most precious possession into the sea was one of the meanest things that she had ever heard. Johnny had arrived back at the Mill soaking wet, shivering and reluctant to say what had happened. Alice, though, had demanded that he tell them what had occurred, and eventually Johnny had relented. Alice too had been angry and had wanted to tell Mrs Goodman. When Johnny had insisted that nobody else be told, Alice had reluctantly agreed, and had helped Johnny to clean and dry the clarinet.

Neither of them knew that Stella had gone to confront Robert, and as she walked home now she wondered what would happen next. Would Robert tell what she had done and get her into trouble with Dad? Hardly, she thought, because then it would come out about him taking Johnny's clarinet. To say nothing of the cowardice involved in three boys ganging up on one. But if Robert didn't pay her back by reporting her, he might get back at her some other way. Well, let him, she thought. For once in her life she had acted impulsively, and she wasn't sorry. Pleased with her new decisiveness, she picked up her pace and headed home through the deepening dusk.

CHAPTER FOURTEEN

Alice quietly closed her bedroom door behind her and tip-toed across the living room. She didn't want to waken Mam in the adjoining bedroom, but she felt too shaken to remain alone in her room. She rarely had nightmares, but the one she had just experienced had been bad. In the dream she had been pursued by a terrifying man, dressed all in black, and Alice's heart was still racing despite the relief of having woken.

There was no point trying to get to sleep again for a while, and she had decided that a glass of warm milk might help her to settle. Although the Goodman's had a small private kitchen into their living quarters, Alice didn't want to disturb her mother, so now she made for the hotel kitchen.

She tightened the belt of her dressing gown, then stepped out into the passageway leading to the kitchen. She saw by the clock on the wall that it was half past eleven, and she reckoned that at this hour there would be nobody preparing food. When she reached the door, however, she was surprised to see a light shining through the doorframe.

Her curiosity aroused, Alice opened the door and stepped in the kitchen. It was dimly lit, with just a couple of lights on. Alice was taken aback to see Johnny sitting there alone. 'Johnny...what are you doing?'

Johnny indicated a steaming mug that sat on the counter before him. 'Having some cocoa. I couldn't sleep.'

'Oh…right.' Alice could see that Johnny was looking at her with concern.

'Are you…are you OK?' he asked.

'Yes. Well…no…not really. I had an awful nightmare. I just…I thought I'd have some warm milk before trying to sleep again.'

'Good idea. Sit yourself down, I'll heat the milk for you.'

'Thanks, Johnny,' she answered, touched by his response.

He quickly lit a gas jet, then poured milk into a saucepan and set it to heat. 'That will warm up in jig time,' he said. 'Want some sugar to sweeten it?'

'Yes, a little please.' After the horror of the nightmare it was comforting to be looked after, and Alice felt less shaky. The milk warmed quickly, and a moment later Johnny offered her a mug of it. Alice cupped it in her hands and drank gratefully.

'Feel a bit better now?'

'Yeah, thanks.'

He looked at her sympathetically. 'A bad nightmare can really throw you. Do you want to talk about it?'

'It was…it was so scary. This man was chasing me. And when he caught me I tried to scream, but I couldn't make any sound. That was…that was the worst part.'

'I can imagine.'

'I don't know what he was going to do to. But I was so frightened I couldn't get a sound out. And then…and then I woke up.

But even though I knew it was a dream…it felt so real I was really uneasy.'

Johnny nodded. 'That's the thing with nightmares. Even after you wake, they can stay in your head…'

Something about the way Johnny said it made Alice look at him questioningly. 'Do you…do you get them a lot?'

Johnny dropped his gaze. 'Just…just now and again,' he answered quietly.

Alice sensed from his demeanour that he was deliberately playing things down. Her own bad dream suddenly seemed less important, and she looked quizzically at her friend. 'It's OK to talk about it. I won't tell anyone.'

Johnny said nothing, and part of Alice felt that maybe she should back off, and not appear to pry. But Johnny had supported her just now. Surely she owed it to him to support him in the same way? 'You don't have to tell me if you don't want to,' she said. 'But we're friends, Johnny. Aren't we?'

'Yes.'

'Well, friends share their worries. Mam says a worry shared is a worry halved.'

Johnny still said nothing, and Alice thought that maybe it wasn't in his nature to open up. She reached out and touched his arm. 'I'm not being nosy, Johnny. If you don't want to go into it, that's fine.'

Still Johnny said nothing, then he slowly raised his gaze and looked her in the eye.

'My nightmare...it's always the same,' he said softly.

'Yeah?' said Alice encouragingly.

'I'm trying to escape from the orphanage. But just when I'm nearly free, I get caught.'

Alice had read somewhere that dreams can be a distorted version of the thoughts we entertain by day, and Johnny's admission intrigued her. 'So...did you actually try to run away?' she asked.

Johnny quickly shook his head. 'No.'

In the past Johnny had told her very little about St Mary's orphanage, and Alice had respected the fact that he wanted to put it behind him. But now the topic had arisen and she had to pursue it. 'But you weren't happy there?'

'Nobody was happy there. It was a terrible place.'

'Were you tempted to run away?'

'I longed to. But I saw what they did to boys who tried to escape.'

'What...what did they do, Johnny?'

'They flogged them. Shaved their heads. Made an example of them.'

Alice felt sickened. 'They *flogged* them?'

'The Brothers could do anything they liked. There was no-one to stop them.'

'That's...it's almost unbelievable.'

'Believe it. This was nothing like your school, Alice. They beat us all the time.'

'For what?'

'For everything. If they caught you talking, they'd beat you. If they caught you writing in the dormitory, they'd beat you. If you tried to complain about anything, they'd beat you. There was one brother, Brother Kenny, and he always beat the last two boys into the shower.'

'Why did he do that?'

'For not being fast enough.' Johnny held up his hand before Alice could respond. 'I know what you're going to say. No matter how fast everyone moved, someone had to be last and second last.'

'Exactly.'

'Brother Kenny used to laugh and say: "It needn't be you!"'

'That's so nasty. Why was he like that?'

'Because he was an animal,' said Johnny bitterly. 'And because there was no-one to stand up for us. So he knew he'd get away with it.'

'And had you no family anywhere? No aunts or uncles you could turn to?'

'Nobody. I wish I had. I'd love to know more about my ma and da.'

'Have you ever made any enquiries?'

'There was nowhere to enquire. They just told me I was orphaned as a baby and my parents were dead. They always said it like somehow being an orphan was my fault.'

'How could it be your fault, Johnny?'

'I don't know. But they said it like we were to blame for being in St Mary's. So they could do what they wanted. We were just orphans. And orphans are dirt.'

'No person is dirt, Johnny.'

'That's what you think. It's what I think too. But some people look down their noses. They think we're flawed, and we deserve whatever we get.'

'That's horrible.'

'The world is horrible. That's why it has to be changed.'

'Yes…it does,' Alice agreed. She understood better now why Johnny's views were radical. But she still thought it was wrong of Mr O'Shea to put a thirteen-year old boy at risk. And after all that Johnny had been through in St Mary's, he deserved to be shielded from any more suffering. Any doubts she had about going to search O'Shea's house evaporated. *She had to act to protect Johnny.*

She looked at him, then instinctively reached out and squeezed his arm. 'I'm so sorry for what you've gone through. But you're not alone any more. Now you've Stella and me as friends.' She held out her hand. 'Deal?'

Johnny looked at her, then shook her hand. 'Deal,' he said.

CHAPTER FIFTEEN

'OK,' said Stella playfully, 'are you feeling clever?'

'We're always feeling clever!' answered Alice.

'Bursting with brains,' added Johnny.

They were relaxing in the band room at the break in Friday night rehearsals. Johnny looked enquiringly at Stella 'So?'

'So, when does New Year's Day come before Christmas Day?'

Johnny considered the question, eager to solve the puzzle. He glanced over at Alice, but it was obvious that she hadn't figured out the answer.

'Well, it can't be anything to do with Leap Year,' he said musingly. 'Can it?'

Stella grinned and shook her head. 'Nothing to do with that.'

'It *never* happens,' said Alice. 'First you've Christmas, then you've New Year. The answer is never.'

'No, the answer is *every* year,' said Stella.

'How can that be?' asked Johnny.

'New Year's Day is the first of January,' said Stella. 'Christmas Day is December the twenty-fifth. So every year New Year's Day comes before Christmas Day.'

'That's a trick question!' complained Alice.

'Of course it is. But if you're clever, and bursting with brains, you should be able to handle trick questions!'

'Fair enough,' said Johnny. 'You got us.'

He sat back happily in his chair and sipped the sweet-tasting homemade lemonade that Mr Tardelli provided each week during rehearsals. Life was going well at the moment, he thought. In fact, since the incident with Robert and the clarinet, a lot of things had gone his way. He had dried out the instrument after finding it in the shallow waters of the Back Strand, and found to his relief that it still played perfectly. He had opened up to Alice about St Mary's, and had felt better afterwards for having talked about the horrors of the orphanage. He had also continued gathering intelligence for Mr O'Shea, and it was gratifying to carry out his role in the struggle for independence. And despite the arrival in Ireland of hundreds of heavily armed Black and Tans, the war was going well for the rebels.

Earlier in the week three hundred thousand people across the country had gone on a one day general strike, in support of hunger-striking republican prisoners, and the government had capitulated and released eighty-nine prisoners. There had been jubilant celebrations, including a victory march by republicans in Balbriggan. In order to continue his spying role, Johnny had resisted the temptation to attend the march. But feelings had run high, and a local policeman, Sergeant Finnerty, had been shot in the back.

Sergeant Finnerty was being treated in the Mater hospital in Dublin, and Johnny hoped that he recovered well. The RIC might be the enemy, but Johnny knew the sergeant as a decent man, and he didn't like the idea of anyone being shot in the back. Suddenly Johnny's reflections were cut short as Mr Tardelli clapped his hands to end the break.

'All right, boys and girls, back to the music!' he cried.

'But not before our weekly joke,' whispered Alice.

'But first we have our little joke,' said Mr Tardelli. 'So, why did the singer climb a ladder?'

'Why did he climb it, Mr T?' queried Johnny.

'He wanted to reach the high notes!' Mr Tardelli laughed heartily at his joke, and was rewarded with a laugh from the band members.

'I think his jokes are getting worse – if that's possible!' said Stella.

'Oh, I nearly forget,' said Tardelli. 'I have the dates for the May-time Festival. Out slot is seven o'clock on the Saturday night. That's seven pm on Saturday, May the fifteenth. Please take a note of that, it's a very important date.'

Johnny felt his heart sink. It was an honour for the band to be asked to play at the Festival, and he was keen to take part. But Saturday night was one of the busiest times in the Mill, and he wasn't sure if Mrs Goodman would let him off work. He had been hoping the band's slot would be during the day, when it was easier for him to get time off. Mrs Gooodman had given way on the issue of the library. Would she be tempted this time to refuse him, to balance things out and prove she was still the boss?

Before Johnny could consider it any further, Mr Tardelli turned over the sheet music on his music stand.

'All right, everyone. We do "Santa Lucia". With feeling, yes? With *soul*.'

Johnny loved the melody of 'Santa Lucia' and he tried to put his worries about Mrs Goodman aside as he picked up his clarinet. Just then there was a flurry of activity at the back of the band room. Before Mr Tardelli could begin conducting, Father Moore, one of the local curates, approached him. The priest's face was grave, and after a whispered conversation, Mr Tardelli looked shocked and put down his baton.

Johnny was intrigued as the bandmaster made an effort to gather himself, then the Italian cleared his throat and addressed them all.

'I'm sorry to tell you some sad news. Father Moore informs me that Sergeant Finnerty died today in the Mater Hospital.'

There was a gasp in the hall, and Johnny too felt shocked. The band members got to their knees when Mr Tardelli announced that Father Moore would lead a decade of the rosary for the repose of the soul of the dead policeman.

Johnny knelt and prayed along with all the others, his mind riven with confusion. On the one hand a war was being waged, and people on both sides were dying all over Ireland. But he had known Sergeant Finnerty, he had spoken to him in the Mill. And the sergeant hadn't been killed in combat – he had been shot in the back. Johnny wished it didn't have to be like this. Yet he knew that it was no use wishing for a fair, clean fight. It wasn't going to be like that, on either side. And the war was no longer being fought in other places, now the fight had reached Balbriggan.

But thoughts of war were for another time, Johnny decided, and he consciously put them from his mind, closed his eyes and prayed for the soul of Sergeant Finnerty.

The train sped south along the coastline, spewing out plumes of black smoke that rose into the blue of the April sky. Alice gazed out the carriage window at the sunlight glinting on the waters of the Irish Sea. It was exciting to be on a mission, despite her nervousness at what would happen when she got to Mr O'Shea's house in Howth.

It was a week and a half now since she had had copies made of the keys that she found in his hotel room. But she had replaced the originals, so O'Shea would have no idea that anyone had searched his wardrobe.

Since getting up early this morning her emotions had been in turmoil. She was still shocked by the announcement last night of the death of Sergeant Finnerty. She felt guilty too about lying to Mam that she was going into Dublin with some girls from the convent to visit the National Museum. But she had to take advantage of the fact that there was no school on Saturdays and that Stella was spending the day with her father.

Alice felt the train slowing now and she rose from her seat as the engine puffed to a halt at Howth Junction. She alighted onto the platform, then a few moments later boarded another train that took her the short distance to the fishing port of Howth. She had often been to Howth on day trips with Mam and so she confidently made her way down the steps at the station exit and headed for the seafront. A Hill of Howth tram clattered across the bridge over the main road, and Alice watched it pull away on its ascent towards the summit of Howth Head.

She walked along the harbour front, the air alive to the sound of screeching gulls. Alice was barely aware of their raucous cries, however, her mind racing as she turned into a steep cobbled street and began to climb. She knew exactly where she was going, having studied a map of Howth in Balbriggan library. But what would happen when she got to O'Shea's house? He could be at home. He could have a vicious guard dog. He could have nosy neighbours.

Alice tried to put her worries aside. There was only so much that could be planned and after that she would have to improvise. She continued climbing, then came to several streets of cottages. She checked that she had the right street, turned into it and walked down the road. Several children were playing with a spinning top, but she didn't encounter any adults. Still, there was no telling who might be looking out a window, so Alice made sure to walk as though she knew where she was headed.

She surreptitiously checked the house numbers, and found that the last cottage of the terrace matched the address she had for O'Shea. More children were playing a skipping game at this end of the road, and Alice turned to a girl of about seven.

'Have you seen Mr O'Shea this morning?' she asked.

The girl looked at her shyly, then shook her head.

'Anybody see him?' persisted Alice.

'I seen him!' said a red-haired boy with slightly ragged clothes. He had been swinging the skipping rope with a hint of aggression, and now he looked Alice in the eye. 'He's gone to work.'

Alice felt her spirits soar, but she tried not to show her relief.

'Why do you want to know?' asked the boy.

'I've something for him. But if he's not here I'll leave it inside, I have a key.' She moved away before the boy could ask her anything else, reaching into her cardigan pocket for the key as she walked towards the front door. She was just about to insert the key in the lock when she heard an adult voice.

'Excuse me?'

Alice looked around to find that O'Shea's next door neighbour had come out her front door. Alice had been taken by surprise but she forced herself to sound unconcerned. 'Good morning,' she said.

''Morning. Were you looking for Mr O'Shea?'

'Yes. I'm his niece, Peggy,' answered Alice with a lie she had prepared in advance.

'Didn't know he had a niece,' said the woman.

Alice felt her mouth going slightly dry. But she told herself that the woman sounded curious rather than suspicious. The trick would be to sound confident, as though everything was normal.

'Well, when I say niece…I *call* him Uncle Oliver. But he's actually a good friend of my dad.'

'Oh, right.'

Quit while you're ahead, thought Alice. 'Well, I better go inside,' she said. 'I've to leave a message and do some housework – need to earn my pocket money!'

As soon as she said it Alice realised that she might have tripped herself up in trying to be too clever. *Supposing O'Shea already had a housekeeper? Wouldn't his next door neighbour be likely to know that?* She glanced over at the woman, trying to read her expression. The woman held her gaze for a moment then nodded.

'All right, Peggy. Mind yourself.'

Alice nodded back, then let herself in, closing the front door behind her. She felt relieved, then realised that she had forgotten about the possibility of a dog. But there was no sound of barking or growling and no scent of dog in the air.

She paused a moment, thinking back to the encounter with the neighbour. Would the woman mention to O'Shea that she had met Peggy, his non-existent friend's daughter? She might. Then again she might not – O'Shea was away travelling a lot and he wouldn't see his neighbours all that regularly. Even if she did tell him, what of it? There was no reason for him to link the mystery Peggy with a girl from the hotel where he stayed when in Balbriggan. And if she found the contraband that she was here to search for, then it wouldn't matter. In that case, *she* would be confronting *him*.

She moved from the small hallway into the living room. She was struck again by how tidy O'Shea was. The room was modestly furnished, with a couple of water-colour paintings on one wall and a copy of the 1916 Proclamation of Independence mounted above the fireplace. Alice quickly searched the room, making sure to replace everything precisely as she found it. She wasn't sure exactly what she might find, but if she unearthed arms or ammunition she would have evidence that she could use. She went through the room carefully, tapping the floor to see if there were any loose floorboards. Everything was in order, however, and Alice switched her search to the small kitchen.

O'Shea had rinsed the breakfast crockery and left it to drain by the sink, and Alice took care not to disturb it. She went through every press and cupboard in the kitchen, then checked the floorboards. Still there was nothing suspicious. She hoped that she hadn't come all the way to Howth on a wild goose chase as she left the kitchen and entered the bedroom.

Once again O'Shea's neatness was in evidence, with the bed well made and his clothes on hangers in the wardrobe. Remembering how O'Shea had hidden his notebook beneath his underwear back at the Mill, she hoped that he might have done something similar here. But a painstaking examination of the chest of drawers, the wardrobe, and the floorboards revealed nothing incriminating.

Maybe he had stuff hidden in the attic. But how could she gain access to there? Better to leave that as a last resort, she decided, and to check the outside toilet instead. She opened the back door of the cottage and stepped into a small garden that was surrounded by high hedges with a rear gate. Adjacent to the cottage was an outhouse that featured a toilet and a storage place for coal or turf. A quick exploration of the toilet revealed nothing, then Alice turned her attention to the storage area. A long tin bath was stacked on top of a pile of turf. Alice reached up and placed the bath on the ground, then began to remove sods of turf in case anything was hidden underneath the fuel. The dust from the turf filled her nostrils, but she forced herself to continue. Suddenly her hand came in contact with a piece of sacking. Alice paused, her pulse beginning to accelerate. She cleared away more turf, exposing a bundle that had been tightly wrapped. She quickly opened the neck of the hidden sack.

She stood unmoving, elated by her discovery. It was an arms cache of four Webley revolvers, several hundred rounds of ammunition, and about a dozen sticks of dynamite. She thought for a moment, then took out one stick of dynamite. She replaced everything else in the sacking and covered it once more with turf. There was a yard brush against the wall and she used it to sweep the turf dust back into the storage area. Finally she replaced the bath on top of the turf. She took one last look, but everything seemed to be as she had found it.

Satisfied with her work, she slipped the stick of dynamite carefully into the inside pocket of her cardigan. Then she let herself out the back gate and started for home.

CHAPTER SIXTEEN

Stella bit into a lemon iced cake as she looked across the sparkling waters of the River Boyne. She was sitting with her father in a riverside teashop in Drogheda. The cake, she thought, wasn't as good as the maple syrup and pancakes that had been her favourite treat in Canada. Still, she loved spending time like this with Dad, when he was relaxed and out of uniform. They had earlier visited the Hill of Tara and driven along the Boyne Valley. But although Stella was enjoying their day out, a worry niggled at the back of her mind.

She put down the cake and turned to her father. 'Dad, can I ask you something?'

'Not the capitals of South America,' he answered with a smile. 'I'm off duty!'

They sometimes entertained themselves with quizzes, and Stella's excellent memory often allowed her to beat her father when it came to recalling the capitals of obscure countries.

'It's not that,' she answered.

Her father's smile faded. 'What is it, Stella?' he asked gently.

'It's…it's the Black and Tans, Dad.' She could see that he was taken by surprise as he looked at her quizzically.

'What…what about them?'

'Why are they so horrible? How are they allowed to get drunk, and beat people up, and smash their homes?'

Her father looked uneasy. 'I admit they're pretty undisciplined. But something had to be done to support the RIC.'

'But the Tans are turning people against British rule. Isn't that the opposite of what we want?'

'It's…it's complicated, Stella. I don't expect you to understand all the politics.'

Stella felt irritated. 'Come on, Dad! I'm not a toddler any more.'

Her father looked taken aback. 'No…no, you're not,' he said. 'Sorry. All right then, I'll try to explain.'

Stella felt slightly guilty for losing her patience and she reached out and squeezed her father's hand. ' I just want to understand. Some of the girls at school are for the rebels, and I have to know what our argument is.'

'Our argument is that a civilised country needs law and order. The police must be allowed do their job. And I know the Black and Tans aren't disciplined – they're certainly not gentlemen.'

'Lots of the RIC and army aren't gentlemen, Dad. But they don't get drunk and terrorise people.'

'Granted. But while there are some dreadful ruffians in the Tans, they are taking the fight to the rebels. The IRA have been shooting policemen. Attacking remote RIC barracks and having easy victories. They're not finding it so easy since the Tans arrived. And there are thousands more on the way. London is fighting back.'

'But…does that mean the government doesn't mind what the

Tans get up to? Once they can beat the rebels?'

Stella could see that her father was uncomfortable.

'I wouldn't quite put it like that,' he said. 'But guerrilla warfare is a murky business. On both sides. Once you unleash certain forces it can be hard to rein them in again.'

Stella considered this for a moment. 'Then maybe…'

'What?'

'If it takes that much force to keep Ireland in the Empire, Dad, maybe it's not worth it. Maybe they should just let Ireland be independent.'

'It's not that simple. Ireland is at the heart of the Empire. If the government throws in the towel here, where does it pull out of next? India? Hong Kong? Our African colonies?'

'So this will be a fight to the finish?'

'The British Empire stands for law, order, civilised values. We can't turn our backs on that, Stella. So yes, we fight until we win.'

Her father cocked his head to one side and looked at her enquiringly. 'Does that give you some answers for the girls in school?'

Stella was struggling to come to terms with what her dad had said, but she nodded in response. 'Yes,' she said. 'Yes, that gives me some answers.'

Johnny hovered nervously in the lobby of the Mill Hotel. To a casual observer he was tidying the newspapers that were left out for guests to read. In reality, he was waiting for the right moment to approach Mrs Goodman. He could see her sitting at her desk in the office behind reception, talking to Miss Hopkins.

Johnny decided that as soon as Miss Hopkins returned to her duty at the desk he would approach his boss in the privacy of the office. There was a lot riding on the outcome of their conversation, and he tried to calm his racing mind.

His emotions had been in turmoil since this morning, when Canon Byrne, the parish priest, had delivered a strong sermon at Mass. The canon had condemned the killing of Sergeant Finnerty as the first murder in Balbriggan in generations. Johnny had felt genuinely sad for the policeman's family, who were taking his body back for burial in his native county Galway. But part of Johnny felt angry at the canon. It was all very well to talk about the value of human life when someone was killed. But what about the value of human life when people were actually alive? Where was Canon Byrne – and others in authority – when Johnny and his fellow orphans were being beaten and terrorised? Or did human life matter if you had standing as a policeman, but not matter if you were poor and orphaned?

Johnny hadn't shared his thoughts with anyone, but he had left Sunday Mass with his mind in flux, and he still felt a bit unsettled. He saw the receptionist finishing her conversation with Mrs Goodman now and he tried to ready himself. It would be important to get the tone right with his boss. *Not too demanding, but not sounding like a beggar. A hard-working employee making a reasonable request.*

He finished tidying the newspapers, then got his nerve up and approached the reception desk.

'Just want a quick word with Mrs G,' he said.

'Go ahead, Johnny,' Miss Hopkins replied, opening the door in the reception desk to allow him access.

Johnny nodded in thanks, then crossed to the office door and knocked. He saw Mrs Goodman look up in mild surprise from her paperwork, then she gestured for him to come in.

'Yes, Johnny?' she said as he entered and stood before her desk.

'Sorry to disturb you, Mrs Goodman. But I was…I was hoping you could oblige me.'

'Oh? Regarding what?'

'It's the Maytime Festival on the fifteenth of next month. Alice has probably told you about it.'

'She mentioned it, yes.'

'The thing is…our band has been given a slot on the Saturday night. I was hoping that maybe I could get off work for a few hours that night.'

'I'm sorry, Johnny, but that won't be possible.'

'Please, Mrs Goodman. It's a big honour to play in the Festival. I'd love to be part of it.'

'I understand that, Johnny. But playing in the band is a hobby. Working here is your *job*. And I need you to do your job that night.'

'I'd make the hours up. I'd do extra hours and work all the following Sunday.'

'If I want you to decide the roster, Johnny, I'll ask you.'

'I just thought—'

'Don't think. Your job is to work the hours you're given.'

'And I do, Mrs G. I work really hard, you know that.'

Johnny looked at her appealingly. He knew that his boss wasn't
nasty by nature. And she had been big enough to change her mind
and had signed his library forms. But did she feel that she had
lost face on that occasion? And was she now making a point by
insisting on having her way? He prayed that she wasn't and that he
could persuade her to judge this case separately.

'I've never asked for anything like this before. But it would
mean the world if you helped me out.'

He thought that Mrs Goodman's expression had softened a
little, and he waited anxiously.

'I don't normally justify myself to employees,' she said. 'But
under the circumstances, I'll explain. We've a wedding here on
the fifteenth. So it's all hands on deck, and that includes you. I'm
sorry you're missing the concert, but it can't be helped. If you
want to stay working in the Mill – and I've no wish to lose you,
Johnny – but if you work here, your job comes before your hob-
bies. Understood?'

Johnny fought to keep his voice from cracking. 'Understood,'
he said.

'Good lad. Was there anything else?'

'No,' answered Johnny, not trusting himself to say anything further. 'Nothing else.'

CHAPTER SEVENTEEN

'I know what you're up to, so don't bother denying it.' Alice looked at Mr O'Shea, curious to see how he would respond to her challenge. She was dressed for school but had approached O'Shea as he left the dining room of the Mill after breakfast. Alice had told him that she had an urgent message for him, and with the commercial traveller's curiosity aroused, she had lead him to a couple of chairs in a quiet corner of the lounge.

Now he looked her in the eye, his face a mask. 'What would I have to deny?'

'That you're involved with the rebels.'

'You're letting your imagination run away with you, Alice. I've a full-time job with Glentoran Whiskey.'

Alice carefully raised her schoolbag and opened it. She tilted the bag so that O'Shea could see the top of the stick of dynamite among her schoolbooks. 'From your cottage,' she said. She was rewarded with a look of shock.

'Now will you take me seriously?' she asked.

'What the hell are you playing at?!'

'I'm not playing. I took that to prove I'd found your hiding place in Howth, so we wouldn't waste time on lies.'

Alice saw O'Shea's expression going from disbelief to fury. 'You snooping brat!'

'I'm sorry, but I had to get proof.'

O'Shea lowered his voice but spoke threateningly. 'Have you *any idea* what you're getting into?!'

Alice had prepared herself for the fact that he would be angry and she didn't falter. 'Calm down, Mr O'Shea. If I'd wanted to go to the police I'd have gone already.'

She saw that he recognised the logic of this and she quickly continued. 'I know the other thing you're doing here in the Mill.'

'Really? What's that?'

'Gathering information on the army and the RIC.'

O'Shea's eyes narrowed. 'Who told you that?'

'It wasn't Johnny, if that's what you're thinking. You gave the game away yourself. I saw you eavesdropping on RIC officers, so I checked out your room.'

'By God, you've some neck!'

Alice ignored O'Shea's indignation and kept going. 'I found your hidden notebook – with Johnny's name in it. It's not right to involve a boy in all this.'

'But it's all right for you to be involved? It's all right for you to search my room, break into my home?!'

'I'm sorry I had to do that. But Johnny needs to be protected. He's had a really hard life up to now, he doesn't deserve any more problems.'

'Anything Johnny's done, he wanted to do.'

'Because he looks up to people like you. But Johnny's my

friend, and I don't want to see him getting hurt. So you better make him stop.'

'Are you threatening me?'

Alice steeled herself and held O'Shea's gaze. 'Yes, I am. End Johnny's part in all this, or else.'

'Or else what?'

'The RIC will be paying a visit to Howth. Or maybe even the Tans.'

Alice saw a flash of anger in O'Shea's eyes, but he controlled it and spoke softly as he drew closer.

'A lot of people are being shot, Alice. I wouldn't like you to be one of them. But you're playing a very dangerous game.'

Alice felt her heart pounding but she forced herself to sound brave. 'You're playing a dangerous game too, Mr O'Shea. I've told nobody any of this stuff. *So far.*'

'You'd be wise to keep it that way. You know what happens informers, don't you? And a kid who informs is still an informer.'

'I'm not an informer. But Johnny's not a soldier. Give me your word that he's out of it, and I'll say nothing. Do we have a deal?'

O'Shea seemed to consider for a moment, then nodded.

'Yes, we've a deal. And here's what it is. When we win this war – and we will win – debts will be settled. Squealers and rats will be remembered. Their homes will be burned to the ground – in accidents. Their businesses will be burned – in accidents. Some of them might be trapped in those burning buildings. That's if they haven't already had accidents because of their treachery. I'm sure you love your mother, Alice, and don't want to ruin her life. So you'll see what's the smart thing to do, when you think this over.'

O'Shea suddenly stood up, then bent down and spoke softly into Alice's ear.

'The only reason I'm giving you this chance is 'cause you're a kid. So we never had this conversation. You were never near my house. And you never speak a word of this to Johnny. That's the deal, Alice. Count yourself lucky to be alive to take it.'

Without another word O'Shea took the stick of dynamite from her schoolbag, slipped it into his pocket, then turned away and walked towards the door.

Alice watched him go, her pulses racing madly. She wiped away the tiny beads of perspiration that had formed on her forehead and wondered how her plan had gone so badly wrong.

CHAPTER EIGHTEEN

'Try that for size!' said Stella, handing Johnny a mug of cocoa.

'Thanks,' he said, taking the beverage and sipping it appreciatively.

'What Mrs Goodman doesn't know won't worry her,' added Stella. Normally she wouldn't be allowed to have Johnny in her hotel room. But Mrs Goodman was gone out for the evening with Alice, to meet relatives who were visiting Dublin.

Stella knew that Johnny had been very disappointed to be refused time off for the Maytime Festival, and she had tried to cheer him up by suggesting an impromptu music session in her room. It was a wet evening, and with a coal fire burning in the grate they sat cosily in chairs in front of the hearth.

Stella really liked the combined sound of her violin and Johnny's clarinet. They had played popular tunes like 'Give my Regards to Broadway', and 'For Me and my Gal', and now Johnny lowered his mug of drinking chocolate and took up the clarinet again.

'Here's one we used to do in St Mary's,' he said.

Stella immediately recognised the lilting tune 'O Solo Mio'. She cupped her mug tightly in her hands, trying to control her emotions. Johnny played on, and Stella turned away slightly, not wanting her friend to be aware of the effect the song was having on her. She hadn't heard it for some time, but the haunting melody brought emotions welling up, and she fought to hold back her tears.

Johnny performed it well, and despite her best efforts, Stella felt the tears rolling down her cheeks. She moved to wipe them away with her hand, but Johnny must have seen her from the corner of his eye, because he stopped playing abruptly.

'Stella…what's…what's wrong?'

'I'm sorry, I…I…'

'What is it?' he asked gently.

'I'm sorry to blubber…it's just…that song reminds me of my brother. He used to love it.'

'Ah, Stella. I'm really sorry.'

'It's OK,' she said, taking out her handkerchief and dabbing her eyes.

'What was…what was your brother's name?'

'George. Georgie Porgy, my dad used to call him.'

Johnny looked at her sympathetically. 'How old was he when he had the accident?'

'He'd just turned seven.'

'God, that's awful. Were you…were you close?'

Stella nodded. 'I remember the day he was born. Even though I was three years older we played a lot together.'

'That must have been good,' said Johnny softly. 'I wish I had a brother – even for seven years.'

'Yeah…' Stella felt her eyes welling up again and she quickly wiped them dry.

'Sorry, Stella. I didn't mean to upset you.'

'It's not your fault.'

Johnny reached out and touched her arm. 'I'm still sorry.'

Something about his concern really moved her, and Stella felt an overwhelming urge to tell him the truth about George. 'You're not the one to blame, Johnny.'

'Sometimes no-one is,' he answered. 'Bad things just happen.'

'Yeah. But sometimes…sometimes people let them happen.' Stella felt a sob in her voice, but she couldn't stop herself now. 'I…I let something terrible happen my brother. And it still…it breaks my heart.'

'But Alice said your brother died in an accident.'

'He was killed by a bear.'

'Yeah? She didn't say that.'

'We were on holidays in the Rockies, and I brought George for a walk on one of the trails. We must…we must have come between a bear and her cubs I think, because…because this black bear suddenly came roaring at us.'

'What did you do?'

'We ran for our lives. We were so scared.'

'But…but George didn't make it?'

Stella fought hard to hold back her sobs. 'No…George didn't make it. The bear…' Suddenly she was wracked with tears and couldn't go on. She saw Johnny rising from his chair, then felt his arm around her.

'It's OK, Stella. It's OK, you don't have to talk about it.' Stella allowed herself to be comforted, then brought her sobbing under control and turned to face Johnny.

'I...I want to talk about it.'

'OK, then,' he said slowly. 'If you're sure.'

'Everyone says it wasn't my fault, Johnny. And I shouldn't feel guilty. But if I hadn't run faster than George, maybe he'd be alive. I was so frightened I wasn't thinking straight – but I still ran off.'

'Most people would.'

'And leave their brother to die? That's what girls in my school in Toronto said, that I left my brother to die.'

'They'd no right to say that, Stella. No right.'

'Lots of them did though. And others probably thought it. I had to be taken out of school, I had a...I'd a sort of nervous break-down.'

'That's dead unfair. Those girls weren't there. In the heat of the moment, most people would have done the same as you.'

'Do you really believe that?'

'Yeah, I do. And supposing you hadn't run faster than George? Supposing you'd run at the same speed and the bear caught you both? It wouldn't have helped George if you died too, would it?'

'I suppose not.'

Johnny looked her firmly in the eye, but spoke softly. 'I've one more question. But it needs a really honest answer. Will you prom-ise to tell the truth?'

Stella had no idea what was coming, but she had gone this far and she would see it out. 'OK, I promise,' she said.

'All right, here it is. If George had run faster than you, and he got away – would you blame him?'

Stella was about to answer, but Johnny raised a hand to stop her. 'Don't answer at once. Really think it through.'

Stella closed her tear-filled eyes and forced herself to revisit that awful day. She tried to imagine the terror or being attacked herself, but George escaping. After a long moment she opened her eyes again and looked at Johnny.

'So, would you have blamed George if he got away?'

'No, I wouldn't.'

'Certain?'

'Absolutely.'

'Well, if you wouldn't blame George for escaping, don't blame yourself for the same thing.'

'I…I'd never thought of it like that.'

'It's the only way that makes sense, Stella. You wouldn't blame him, and I'm sure – wherever he is now – he doesn't blame you.'

Johnny's words felt like a balm, and Stella looked at him fondly. She could hardly believe that the conversation had taken this turn, but a burden had been lightened. 'Thanks, Johnny,' she said. 'Thank you so much.'

'Instead of thanking me, promise me one more thing.'

'What?'

'Next time you think about it, remember what I said. About you not blaming George, and George not blaming you.'

'OK, I will.'

'Promise?'

Stella dabbed her eyes a final time. 'OK, Johnny. That's a promise.'

CHAPTER NINETEEN

The choppy waters of the Irish Sea shimmered in the late April sunshine. A warm breeze was blowing, carrying the tang of salt and capping the waves with white foam, but Johnny barely noticed as he strode along the coastal track. He was dressed in his Sunday clothes for a visit to Mr Tardelli's cottage on the northern outskirts of town, and his mind was racing as he considered the bandmaster's invitation.

After Friday night's rehearsal Mr Tardelli had called him aside and asked him for tea on Sunday afternoon. So far as Johnny knew, none of the other band members had ever been invited to the cottage, and he was curious to know what was behind the invitation.

He turned off the track now and opened the gate leading up the path to the thatched cottage. It was a small house, but the whitewashed walls were freshly painted, the thatch was well maintained, and it had a good sea view.

Johnny knocked on the hall door, and a moment later Mr Tardelli opened it and smilingly ushered him in.

'Johnny, you're very welcome.'

'Thanks, Mr T.'

'Take a seat, please. Later we have tea, but for now I've got some lemonade, OK?'

'Lemonade is always good,' said Johnny with a grin as he sat at the living room table. The room was slightly dark because of the small cottage windows. But it was nicely furnished, with brightly coloured paintings of Mediterranean scenes that Johnny assumed were of Mr Tardelli's home place of Sardinia. The living room was a little cluttered, with sheet music stacked on the mantlepiece and on several of the chairs, but everything was clean, and there was a comfortable, lived-in feel to the place.

Johnny drank the lemonade, savouring its cool sweetness as the Italian joined him at the table and poured himself a glass of red wine.

'So, I'm sure you wonder why I ask you here, Johnny?'

'Well, yes.'

'For tea, like I said. And perhaps later we listen to some music, if you like.'

'That would be grand.'

'But first I need to tell you something, and ask you something.'

'OK,' said Johnny, his curiosity mounting.

'What I want to tell you is that you're a very talented musician.'

'Oh. Well, thanks, Mr T…'

'You're the best in the band. Easily, the best.'

'Thank you,' said Johnny, feeling pleased but also slightly embarrassed. When he had played the clarinet in St Mary's any praise for his musicianship had been limited, grudging even. It was exciting now, if a little disconcerting, to be praised so openly.

'So what I wanted to ask, Johnny, was if you ever think of becoming a professional musician?'

Johnny was taken aback. Playing music for a living was a dream that he had only entertained secretly. To have it suggested by a professional like Mr Tardelli was hugely flattering.

'I've…I've thought about it now and then,' he admitted. 'But I don't know where I'd even start. I've a full-time job in the Mill.'

'But you would like it?'

'I'd love it! More than anything in the world.'

'Then you must make it happen, Johnny.'

'That's easier said than done.'

'*Everything* is easier said than done. But if it's what you want to do with your life, you find a way to do it.'

'You really think that's possible?'

'I *know* it is. I wanted to make music my life. But I lived in Santa Teresa, a small town in Sardinia. I couldn't make a career there, Johnny. But I studied hard. I learnt music. I learnt English. And after many years, many adventures, many setbacks — here I am in Ireland, making my life through music.'

'I'm really glad it worked out for you.'

'Thank you, Johnny. But I can guess what you're thinking now.'

'What's that?'

'That your life is different. And it is. You started in an orphanage. You left at thirteen for a full-time job. They won't even let you off for one night to play in the Maytime Festival. Many problems, Johnny, many challenges. But can I give you a little advice?'

'Of course.'

'Some people have an easy start in life. Some have a tough start. But in the end, everyone has to – what is the word – has to *create*. We each have to *create* a world that we live our lives in. Do you understand?'

'I think so.'

'You had a bad start, Johnny. But you mustn't let that decide the rest of your life. There comes a time to put that all behind you, make a new life. If you do that and work really hard, many things are possible.'

'I'm not afraid of hard work.'

'Good. I know you're not like Alice, or Robert, or Stella. They go to school, you have to work. Maybe you feel sometimes like an outsider, yes?'

'Sometimes.'

'I just want to tell you, that's all right, Johnny. When I came to Ireland I felt like an outsider. Sometimes I still do. But it doesn't stop me. Now I live the life I wanted, a life of music. You could too.'

Johnny took a sip of lemonade, his head spinning.

'You don't mind, Johnny, that I say these things?'

Johnny looked at the Italian and smiled. 'No, Mr T, I don't mind. It's actually…it's the best thing anyone's ever said to me.'

Mr Tardelli smiled back, then raised his wine glass in a toast. 'To being a musician, then,' he said

Johnny clinked glasses. 'To being a musician.'

CHAPTER TWENTY

'I won't change my mind, Alice. Johnny has to work the night of the concert and that's an end to it.'

'Ah, Mam. It's only one night. Just this once can't you replace him?'

Alice looked appealingly to her mother across the table in their living room. They were having tea and biscuits before bedtime, and Alice hoped that in the relaxed end-of-day atmosphere her mother might be persuaded.

'And the next time one of the other staff feels like breezing off somewhere,' said Mam, 'do I replace them too?'

'No, but—'

'No I don't. So I can't make an exception for Johnny. If I did the other staff could start to resent him. Did he put you up to this?'

'No! No, he'd nothing to do with it.'

'Good. Because I explained to him there's a wedding reception that night, and I can't let him off. Not that I should have to explain myself.'

'I know, Mam. It's just...playing in the band means a lot to him.'

'I understand. But his job ought to mean more to him than his hobby. And if you insist on being friends with a member of staff, Alice, then you've got to understand something too.'

'What?'

'That Johnny the person, and Johnny the boots, are one and the same. You can't just separate them when it suits you.'

Alice thought for a moment, then looked her mother in the eye. 'But you do that, Mam.'

'How do I?'

'With Robert. I told you about him throwing the clarinet into the sea and being nasty to Johnny. But you're still nice to him. You separate Robert the bully from Robert the son of Dr Foley.'

Alice could see that her mother looked uncomfortable.

'I…I take your point, Alice. But I've known Robert since he was a baby.'

'He's still a bully. There're times I really hate him.'

'Alice…'

'Well I do. He is a bully, Mam.'

'Perhaps at times. But it's…it's complicated.'

'How is it?'

'Robert is…he's insecure.'

'Insecure?! He's full of himself!'

'In some ways, yes.'

'He thinks he's great. Just because his father's a surgeon, and he's good at rugby.'

'That's only part of it, Alice. His mother died, and he's always…'

'Always what?'

'He's always had to compete for Dr Foley's attention. He's a very good surgeon but not…not the warmest of men. Robert's always tried to win his approval.'

'By what? Picking on someone like Johnny, who's never had half the things Robert has?'

'Robert sees Johnny as a threat.'

'How is he a threat?'

'Everybody likes Johnny. Not everyone likes Robert. And Johnny, by all accounts, is a better musician.'

'So it's OK to make little of Johnny, so he'll feel better?'

'No, it's not. I'm not justifying him, Alice. I'm simply trying to explain that sometimes people behave badly for reasons that aren't obvious. Sometimes the cockiest people are unsure of themselves behind it all.'

'Then Robert should deal with that, and not use Johnny to score points.'

'I agree. And I hope that in time Robert matures. But in spite of all of that, I can't make an exception of Johnny because you've befriended him. So please, Alice, don't ask me again – all right?'

Alice paused, then nodded reluctantly. 'All right.'

Her mother rose. 'I'm going to do a final check around.'

'OK.'

Alice remained at the table, her thoughts whirling. *Who would ever have thought that Robert was insecure? Or secretly jealous of Johnny?* But it seemed now as though everyone had secrets. Stella had told her previously of her brother being killed by a bear, yet it had only come out in the last week that Stella had secretly blamed herself. Alice was glad that her friend had finally unburdened herself, and she wished that she could share her own secret about Mr O'Shea.

O'Shea had ordered her so say nothing to Johnny, however. And Stella might feel conscience-bound to inform Commander Radcliffe, if Alice told her about the arms cache in Howth. Alice had briefly considered alerting the police anonymously after her showdown with O'Shea. But the commercial traveller would guess who had turned him in, which would put herself and Mam in danger. Besides, if O'Shea was arrested Johnny might end up in police custody too. No, thought Alice, better all round to say nothing. She rose from the table and made for her room, resigned to telling no-one of her secret.

Stella's instinct was to attack, but she took her time, carefully studying every piece on the chessboard. Golden May sunlight streamed in the windows of the chess club on this, the final night before the club finished for the summer.

Stella was delighted to have reached the final. Her tactics tonight had been good, and as she studied the board now she felt confident. Her one regret was that her opponent was Johnny.

She had grown to like him a lot, and since the night that they had talked about George's death she felt closer to him than ever. She was particularly grateful for how he had been sympathetic in a practical way that had helped her to move on. There had been no embarrassment on meeting the day after her revelation, and with the burden of secrecy lifted, she had felt able to discuss it with Alice as well.

The one tricky part of her friendship with Johnny was his rebel sympathies. As the daughter of a British officer her loyalties were becoming torn. Instinctively, she had been on the side of the government and the rule of law. Lately though she was offended by the behaviour of the Black and Tans, and swayed by the growing desire of the people for Irish Home Rule. Even the government was finding it hard to resist public opinion, and only yesterday they had released forty hunger striking rebels from prison.

For the most part though she didn't discuss politics with Johnny – it was like an unspoken agreement between them - and their friendship had thrived, despite the worsening conflict.

Now though she wondered if their relationship would be affected were she to beat him in the chess final. Johnny was competitive by nature, and Stella knew he would be disappointed to lose tonight. But boys had won the final eight times in the last ten years, and Stella was eager to get another win for the girls. Glancing up briefly from the board, she caught the eye of Alice among the spectators. Alice gave her a thumbs-up sign. Her friend had even made a placard stating 'Come on, the girls!', which she had playfully displayed before the start of the match.

Stella gave her a quick nod, then returned to the chessboard and made her move. She had tried to work out in her head all the different ways that Johnny could respond, but she reckoned that no matter what he did she had the upper hand.

Johnny considered for a moment, then moved his bishop. Alice realised at once that he had made a tactical error. Her heart soared, yet she resisted the temptation to move in at once for the kill. She knew that Johnny was deeply disappointed to be missing the Maytime Festival next Saturday night. Was it fair to make him lose the chess final as well? Should a true friend sacrifice the pleasure of winning the tournament, and let a victory tonight compensate Johnny for missing out on the festival? Or would he be offended if he suspected that he had been allowed to win?

Stella hesitated. She glanced over at Alice again. Even though her 'Come on, the girls!' sign was playful, Stella suspected that it meant something to her friend to prove that girls could compete successfully with boys. Which meant that if she did Johnny a favour by losing, she might be letting Alice down.

Stella looked at the board as though figuring out her next move. But she knew the move that would bring her victory. And she knew the move that could be passed off as an error, and that would allow Johnny back into the match. She bit her lip, unsure what was the best thing to do. She thought of her father, whose golden rule was that if in doubt, always do what your instincts tell you is right.

Without any further hesitation she reached out and moved her queen. Up to this, Johnny's face had been a mask. Now, however, Stella could see that he knew defeat was inevitable. He reached out slowly and toppled his king in surrender. 'Well played, Stella,' he said slowly, offering his hand. 'Well played.'

'Thanks for a great game, Johnny,' she said, shaking hands.

There was applause from the spectators, and Stella nodded in acknowledgement. She was excited by her win, then she looked at Johnny, and despite herself, she couldn't help but feel a little sad.

CHAPTER TWENTY-ONE

The ruins of Gormanston RIC station smouldered in the warm May sunshine. Johnny, Alice and Stella lowered their bicycles onto the nearby grass verge and joined the other onlookers who had taken a Sunday stroll to view the burnt-out barracks.

It had been set ablaze by the IRA the previous night, and Johnny was gratified that the rebels were becoming ever more active, despite the presence of the Black and Tans. The last couple of weeks had been an emotional roller-coaster, with the disappointment of losing the chess final and missing the Maytime Festival partly offset by rebel successes, and by his own intelligence gathering.

While working at the wedding reception in the Mill he had overheard a drunken officer let slip that the air base at Gormanston was earmarked to be a major centre for the Black and Tans. Mr O'Shea had thanked him for the information, saying it confirmed existing suspicions, and Johnny had been pleased to feel useful. He had sensed a certain wariness in the commercial traveller, however, and wondered if O'Shea was becoming rattled by thousands of Tans being recruited and pouring into Ireland.

Johnny knew that it would certainly change things around Balbriggan when the Tans took over the former RAF base, but that was a worry for another time. Today he would savour the symbolism of the burnt down barracks and then enjoy the planned picnic with his friends.

'Right,' said Alice. 'There's only so long you can look at a burntout ruin. Will we push on?'

'Yes, I've seen enough,' answered Stella.

'Johnny?'

'Fine.'

They returned to the grass verge and the two girls mounted their bicycles. Johnny swung his leg over the crossbar of the bicycle that he had borrowed from Mikey, the porter – this time with Mikey's permission. They cycled along country lanes, the hedgerows heavy with white-flowering Hawthorne. After several miles they came to their favourite picnic spot at a grassy bank beside a rippling stream.

Johnny and Stella spread a blanket on the ground while Alice unpacked the picnic baskets that she and Stella had carried on their bicycles.

'We won't go hungry, anyway,' said Johnny, grateful for Alice's interest in cookery and food.

'No point living in a hotel if you can't get your hands on grub!' she answered. She placed three bottles of lemonade in the shallow waters of the stream to cool, then began unwrapping sandwiches, fruit, cake and biscuits.

'We'll never move after eating all this,' said Stella.

'Hey, that reminds me,' said Alice. 'Why couldn't the teddy bear finish his dessert?

Johnny usually liked Alice's jokes and he looked at her expectantly. 'Why couldn't the teddy bear finish his dessert?'

'Because he was stuffed!'

Everybody laughed, then Alice indicated the sandwiches. 'Help yourselves. By the time we finish the sambos the lemonade will be cooler, and we can have it with our cakes.'

Johnny tucked into a delicious chicken sandwich and everyone fell quiet as they enjoyed the food. There was a sweet scent of gorse in the air, the sun shone down from a clear blue sky, and Johnny felt at peace.

After a few moments Alice looked at the others. 'Isn't summer just the best season?' she said.

'Gets my vote,' agreed Johnny.

'Mine too,' said Stella. 'Except…well, except that once school ends, we'll all be split up for the summer.'

'I hadn't thought of it that way,' answered Alice. 'Still, when you get to Canada you'll see your Mam and your Granddad again.'

'Yes, that part will be good.'

'But…but you're still a bit wary?' asked Johnny gently.

'Less so now,' said Stella. 'Yourself and Alice have been great. I feel much better about going back since I…well, since I told you about George.'

'Good,' said Johnny.

'Yeah, that's what friends are for,' agreed Alice.

'So what about you two?' queried Stella. 'What are your plans?'

'Mam and I will go to Parknasilla as usual,' said Alice. 'I'll get to spend two whole weeks with my cousins.' She pulled a face, and the others laughed. 'Actually, they're not that bad. But it's not as exciting as crossing the Atlantic.'

'And what about you, Johnny?' asked Stella.

'I might go to New Orleans and meet some jazz musicians,' he answered playfully.

'Seriously though?' said Stella.

Johnny shrugged. 'I'm not sure how much time off I get. But I'll probably do some day trips.' *And maybe I'll get some extra missions as things hot up with the Black and Tans,* he thought. But even though they had just viewed the burnt-out RIC station, today felt like a day off from all the strife, and Johnny decided to put the war from his mind. 'I'll play it by ear,' he said.

'Anyway we've another whole month before school breaks up,' said Alice. 'Let's just enjoy our time together.'

'I'll drink to that. Or I would if I had a bottle of lemonade!' said Johnny.

Alice reached into the stream, withdrew the three bottles and gave one each to Stella and Johnny. 'To our time together,' she said.

All of them tapped their bottles together laughingly. 'To our time together!'

CHAPTER TWENTY-TWO

Stella tried not to fidget as she watched her father finishing his paperwork for the day. They were seated in the rooms of the commanding officer in Gormanston, and the plan was that once Dad finished they would have dinner in the Mill. Recently her father had spent much of his time training his squadrons in RAF Baldonnel, and Stella was eager to take the chance to talk on a rare day when he finished work early.

A hazy sun shone in through the barracks window, bathing the room with golden light, but Stella was too preoccupied to enjoy the mellow May evening. She watched her father now, biding her time. He closed the file that he was reading and started to tidy his desk. Now was the moment, she knew, and she looked directly at him. 'Dad, can I ask you something?'

'Of course.'

'Is the war with the rebels going to take a long time?'

'Well…it may take a while. Why do you ask?'

'I was wondering if we'll still be here next year.'

'I'm pretty sure we'll still be in Ireland. But I'll be stationed full time in Baldonnel by then.'

Stella looked at him, struggling to find the right words. 'The thing is…I really don't want to move school, Dad. I've friends here now. I'd hate leaving them and having to start again.'

'Well, where we'd live isn't decided, Stella. A lot depends on what happens with Granddad's health, and when Mom can come back. I'll have my quarters in Baldonnel, of course, but Mom would want to rent a house.'

'Could we rent around here again? So I can stay in my school?'

'Possibly. But it's a fair drive from here to Baldonnel. Probably make more sense to rent a house nearer to there.'

'I'd hate not seeing Alice and Johnny, and the other girls in school. It's hard, Dad, being the new girl.'

'Yes, I understand that.'

'So could I stay on in the Mill?'

Her father didn't answer at once, and Stella studied his face, anxious for any clue to his thinking.

'If Mom can't come home by the autumn, then yes, I suppose you could. Assuming that's all right with Mrs Goodman.'

'That won't be a problem. It's business for her, and I'm company for Alice.'

'Quite. But If Mom returns and we rent a house that's different. Not much point renting a house in Balbriggan when I'm gone from Gormanston.'

'But even if you rented a house in Dublin, or out towards Baldonnel, couldn't I still stay here at the Mill?'

'I imagine Mom would prefer you to stay in the family home, Stella.'

'And I would – at weekends, and all the summer holidays, and Easter and Christmas. But loads of people go to boarding school.

You did yourself, Dad. This would be just like boarding school, except that I'm boarding with Alice's family.'

Her father looked thoughtful again, then nodded. 'I suppose there's a certain logic in that.'

Stella felt her spirits soaring. 'So I can stay then?'

'Yes, if that's what you really want.'

Stella rose from the seat and hugged her father. 'Thanks, Dad, that's great!'

He kissed her forehead. 'Whatever makes you happy, Stella'.

'This does! Alice is great, she's the best friend I've ever had.'

'Yes, she's a lovely girl.'

'And eh…that's the other thing I wanted to ask.'

'What?'

Stella gathered her nerve, then looked at her father appealingly. 'Seeing as you think she's lovely, and because she's my best friend…could she keep me company? On our holidays?'

'You mean–'

'Could she come to Canada? Please, Dad. Could she?'

Mr O'Shea strolled out of the dining room of the Mill, and Alice dodged him by slipping into a corner of the lounge. Since their confrontation she had avoided him as much as possible, though they greeted each other politely when their paths crossed. She hadn't discussed O'Shea's secret with anyone in the weeks since her trip to Howth. But O'Shea had previously seemed decent, and she still wasn't sure if his threat to her life was real, or if it was just to scare her into silence. Either way she had followed his order and said nothing to anybody, including Johnny.

Was that cowardice on her part? She *could* defy O'Shea and try to persuade Johnny to give up his dangerous role. But if O'Shea's threats were real she would be putting herself and Mam at risk. And Johnny might be angry with her for meddling. She sometimes thought, too, of the lives that could be lost through the use of the weapons O'Shea had stockpiled. Then again, the Crown forces were even more heavily armed, and in spite of everything, she couldn't bring herself to turn in O'Shea to the Black and Tans.

She waited in the lounge now until O'Shea had ascended the stairs, then she walked back towards the lobby, her thoughts still in a whirl. Before she could think about it any more, Stella burst in through the main entrance, followed by Commander Radcliffe.

'Alice, the very person!' she cried.

'What have I done now?' asked Alice.

'Nothing – well, not yet. But I've great news. Well, great if you want it, that is.'

Alice laughed. 'Stella, I've no idea what you're talking about!'

'Dad says you can come to Canada with us for the holidays. If you'd like.'

Alice could barely believe her ears. 'If I'd like?! Do ducks swim?!'

'It would be for six weeks.'

'Brilliant – provided Mam agrees. Let's ask her now!'

'OK.'

Alice was about to move off when she remembered her manners and turned to Stella's father. 'Thank you, Commander Radcliffe. Thank you so much.'

'A pleasure, Alice.' he answered, before raising a hand in warning 'Though as you say, it's up to your mother.'

'Come in with us then,' said Alice. 'She'll take it more seriously when she sees that you're on for it.'

Without waiting for a reply Alice lead the way to the family's quarters. 'Mam!' she cried, 'Mam!'

'What's all the shouting about?' her mother asked as she came into the living room. 'Oh, Commander Radcliffe, Stella,' she said in surprise.

'Forgive our intrusion,' said Stella's father. 'But Alice insisted we join her.'

'Please, take a seat. Can I offer you some tea?'

'Thank you, no, we're about to have dinner,' said Commander Radcliffe.

Alice was bursting with impatience but she knew better than to interrupt Mam until hospitality had been offered.

'If you're sure?' said her mother.

'Absolutely,' answered Stella's father. 'Thank you all the same.'

'Mam, Commander Radcliffe and Stella have invited me to go with them to Canada!'

'My goodness.'

'I hope you don't think it an impertinence, Mrs Goodman,' said

Stella's father.

'Not at all. But it is a surprise.'

'But isn't it a brilliant surprise, Mam?! Can I go? *Please?*' Alice found herself holding her breath as her mother considered the request.

'What about Parknasilla?' she said. 'Your cousins are expecting you.'

'I saw them last year, Mam. And the year before. And I'll probably see them next year. But this is the chance of a lifetime.'

Alice sensed that her mother was swayed, but still uncertain.

'Please, Mrs Goodman,' added Stella. 'Alice has been a brilliant friend. It would mean the world to me if she came along.'

Alice swallowed hard, praying that Stella's appeal might tip the balance. There was a brief pause, then her mother spoke. 'I suppose Parknasilla will still be there next year.'

'Does that mean I can go?' asked Alice.

'As you say, it's the chance of a lifetime. And a very kind offer. So yes, you may go.'

Alice whooped with joy, then she hugged her mother, Stella, and even Commander Radcliffe. All her worries about Mr O'Shea were temporarily banished, by this, the most exciting offer she had ever had.

CHAPTER TWENTY-THREE

Johnny kept his distance from Robert as the band members spilled out of the train at Bray station. Each year Mr Tardelli brought them on an outing before the band broke up for summer, and this year their destination was the lively seaside resort of Bray, in county Wicklow.

Now that the school holidays had started in Clongowes, Robert was back home, and had rejoined the band. Since the incident with the clarinet there had been a shift in his attitude, and he seemed less cocky now. Johnny wondered if perhaps he regretted trying to impress his schoolmates by throwing the clarinet into the sea. But if he was sorry for what he had done he hadn't been big enough to apologise, and Johnny kept his dealings with him to a bare minimum.

Stella was cooler with him too, Johnny had noted, and it fell to Alice to play the role of the go-between, chatting to all of them during the thirty-five mile rail journey south to Bray. Now everybody milled around in high spirits as Mr Tardelli did a head count before leaving the train station.

'Everybody stay together, please. But if anyone gets lost we meet here for the six o'clock train home. Any questions?'

'I've a question, Mr Tardelli,' said Alice. 'Why can't your nose be twelve inches long?'

The band leader smiled. 'Eh…because my name isn't Pinocchio?'

'No, if your nose was twelve inches long – it would be a foot!'

Everybody laughed, and Mr Tardelli nodded good humouredly. 'Very good, Alice, very good. And now, we go to the seafront.'

Johnny fell into step beside Stella as the group made its way along the Albert Walk, a narrow passageway lined with shops selling postcards of the resort, alongside buckets, spades and other seaside accoutrements.

'Ever been to Bray before?' asked Johnny.

'No, but I heard it's great.'

'It's brilliant. They've paddle boats, and chairoplanes, and fairy floss, and Punch and Judy shows.'

'Sounds good.'

'And as for the fish and chips.' Johnny licked his lips playfully. 'The best in the world!'

They reached the end of Albert Walk and turned left to reach the Promenade that ran along the waterfront. There were fluffy white clouds in a blue sky, and the sea sparkled, while at the end of the bay Bray Head rose steeply to a peak of almost eight hundred feet.

'Nice, isn't it?' said Johnny.

'Lovely.'

The resort was crowded with day trippers, but it made for a lively atmosphere, and Johnny's group crossed the road and began to make their way along the sunlit Promenade. After a moment Johnny saw a commotion ahead as strollers slowed, and others turned and walked back the way they had come.

'Tans!' said Alice, who was at the front of their group.

Mr Tardelli raised a hand and the band members straggled to a halt. Johnny moved to join Alice and saw that six heavily armed Tans were blocking the Promenade. They were questioning people, and two of them were man-handling a youth in his late teens. Johnny realised that the men were drunk, and he sensed that this was less a security check and more an exercise in blackguardism.

'All right, everybody, we go a different way,' said Mr Tardelli.

'Half a mo, mate, half a mo!' cried one of the Tans as he lumbered over to the band members.

He was a heavily built man with crooked teeth and a glassy look in his eyes. 'Who says you're going anywhere?'

'I'm with a group of children, they can't interest you.'

'*They can't interest me*,' said the Tan, mocking Mr Tardelli's Italian accent. 'I'll decide what interests me, Antonio.'

Mr Tardelli kept his voice calm but looked the man in the eye. 'My name is not Antonio.'

'Really?' said the Tan. Suddenly he grabbed Mr Tardelli by the lapels and pulled him forward until their faces were just inches apart. 'Your name is what I decide to call you. Understood?'

Johnny could see that the band leader was shaken.

'Understood, Antonio?' repeated the Tan threateningly.

Johnny saw Mr Tardelli swallowing nervously, then the Italian spoke. 'My name is Mario Tardelli.'

'Oh. Got a smart one, have we?' said the Tan, his voice slurred by drink. He shook Mr Tardelli, then pulled his face close again. 'We know how to deal with smart blokes. Bert!' called the Tan to one of his comrades, 'hold this geezer while I put manners on him.'

'My pleasure, Fred, my pleasure,' answered his friend, shouldering his rifle and approaching.

Johnny knew that the Tans were capable of really vicious beatings, and before he realised what he was doing he spoke up. 'Leave him alone!' he cried. 'He's done nothing wrong.'

The Tan holding Mr Tardelli released him and swung round aggressively to confront Johnny. '*Leave him alone?*' He repeated. 'Who the hell are you to give orders?'

'Cheeky little pup!' said the second Tan, 'I'll give you what for!'

Johnny felt a stab of fear as the second man grabbed him. The Tan raised his hand threateningly, but Robert suddenly stepped forward. 'No!' he cried, standing beside Johnny. 'Let him go.'

The second Tan had been surprised but now he held onto Johnny but turned to Robert. 'Do you want a hiding too, son?'

'None of us want a hiding,' said Robert. 'None of us want any trouble. We just want to go on our way.'

'Should have thought of that before Antonio here got smart,' said the first Tan.

Johnny felt relieved to have avoided the blow from the Tan, and was amazed that Robert had backed him up. But all of the Tans seemed drunk, and this could still end badly.

'Ain't that right, Antonio?' asked the Tan.

Still Mr Tardelli refused to answer to the insulting nickname, and Johnny admired his courage but feared for his safety.

'Leave the kids for now, Bert,' said the first Tan. 'Time for an Italian lesson!'

The second Tan let Johnny go and moved towards Mr Tardelli. Johnny caught a movement from the corner of his eye, then to his surprise Stella strode forward and addressed the first Tan.

'I suggest you stop right now,' she said. Her voice sounded well educated and authoritative, and she was expensively dressed, and Johnny could see that the Tans were taken aback.

'My father is a British officer, and a decorated war veteran,' Stella continued. 'He was commander of Gormanston Camp and now he's the senior officer at RAF Baldonnel. He's only to lift the phone to speak to your superior officers. So I think the best thing all round is if we go on our way, and you go on yours. All right?'

Johnny was astonished by Stella's coolness, but he could see that the first Tan still wanted trouble.

'I don't take orders from some little dolled up toff,' he said.

'Naw. Drop it, Fred, ain't worth it,' said the second Tan.

The first Tan looked at the band members, his gaze still glassy and hostile. Johnny sensed, however, that even in his drunken state he knew better than to challenge the social order that Stella had called into play.

'You watch your step in future,' he warned, releasing Mr Tardelli. 'Next time you won't get off so easy.' With that he turned away, and the Tans moved on down the Promenade.

'I'm so sorry about that, Mr Tardelli,' said Stella.

'In every country they have idiots and thugs,' he said sadly. Then he brightened and gave a little bow. 'But thank you, Stella. Thank you very much. And also Johnny and Robert. Brave boys.'

Johnny nodded in acknowledgement, relieved that Stella's intervention had saved them all. But while her actions had surprised him, it was Robert's move to support him that was truly amazing. He thought again of how Robert's demeanour had been less arrogant lately, and wondered if his support was Robert's way of apologising for the clarinet incident. Whatever the reasoning, he had been courageous, and Johnny turned now to the other boy. 'Thanks, Robert,' he said.

Robert held his gaze a moment, then nodded. 'You're grand.'

'All right, boys and girls!' called Mr Tardelli. 'We've had a little excitement. Now I think we cool down with a swim, then have some fish and chips. All in favour say "Aye".'

Johnny happily joined the others in shouting 'Aye!'

CHAPTER TWENTY-FOUR

Alice thought this was one of the most thrilling moments of her life. The car was coming that would carry herself, Stella and Commander Radcliffe to Dublin, from where they would cross to Liverpool and get the transatlantic liner to Canada.

She stood in the bright July sunlight outside the entrance to the Mill, being seen off by Mam, Johnny, Robert, Dr Foley, Mrs Nagle, the cook, and Mr Byrne, the barman. Mikey Power, the porter, had their trunks and cases ready on the pavement.

Alice's emotions had been fluctuating since having breakfast earlier with Mam. She knew that her mother was struggling to hold back the tears when giving last minute advice over breakfast on how to behave during the six weeks away with the Radcliffes. Alice herself had felt emotional, and had hoped that she wouldn't get homesick. She had hugged Mam and told her that she would miss her. But even though she had felt a sudden surge of affection for Mam, she had also been thrilled to be setting off on such a big adventure.

Now, as a staff car with an RAF driver pulled in to the kerb, it was time to set off. Yet even in this moment of excitement the presence of a military vehicle reminded her of the turmoil she was leaving behind. In the last couple of weeks the war had worsened dramatically in Ulster, with hundreds of Catholic workers driven from the Harland and Wolffe shipyard in Belfast, and seventeen people killed during fighting in Derry.

But sad as it was that anyone should be killed, Alice's biggest worry was closer to home. With the RIC and the army clashing more frequently with the IRA, how long would it be before Johnny got discovered as a spy? So far Alice had obeyed Mr O'Shea's warning and given Johnny no inkling that she knew about his secret. But anything could happen in the next six weeks, and she wished now that she had had the courage to defy O'Shea and to warn Johnny to stop risking his life.

Before she could think about it any further, Mam approached and gave her a final hug. 'Bye, Darling.'

'Bye, Mam.'

'Write often, and say your prayers every night.'

'I will.'

Mrs Nagle, who was always dramatic, had tears in her eye as she bid Alice farewell, and Alice gave her a quick hug. 'It's all right, Mrs Nagle, I'll be back in six weeks!'

'God willing, Alice, God willing.'

Dr Foley shook hands and wished her well, and Robert followed suit. Mikey Power loaded the luggage into the car, and while Mam and the Foleys were saying goodbye to Stella and Commander Radcliffe, Alice found herself alone with Johnny.

'Have a great trip, Alice,' he said, offering his hand and smiling warmly.

Alice shook his hand. Just for the moment everyone else was distracted, and acting on impulse, Alice suddenly drew nearer to him and spoke softly. 'Be careful, Johnny. I know what you're doing with Mr O'Shea. It's really dangerous. Try and get out of it. And if you can't get out of it, please, please be careful.'

Johnny looked shocked, but before he could respond, Commander Radcliffe called out light-heartedly, 'Chocks away, Alice! Time to go!'

'Coming.' Alice gave Johnny's arm a quick squeeze, then she turned away, crossed the pavement to the staff car, and climbed into the back beside Stella.

Commander Radcliffe was sitting in the front seat and he nodded to the driver, who let off the brake and began to pull away. There was a last flurry of waving and goodbyes, and Alice and Stella twisted round in the back seat to continue waving out the rear window. Alice could see that Johnny still looked shocked. Had she done the right thing in showing her hand? She hoped so, both for Johnny and for herself and Mam. Then the car turned a bend and everyone was lost to view. *Nothing more I can do about it for the next six weeks*, she thought.

'Well, roll on, Canada!' said Stella.

Alice tried to banish her worries, and she smiled at her friend. 'Roll on, Canada!'

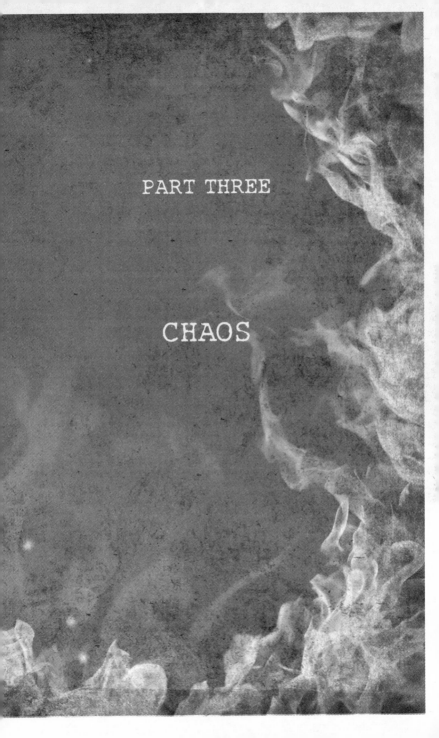

PART THREE

CHAOS

CHAPTER TWENTY-FIVE

Johnny worked contentedly in the yard of the Mill, stacking empty stout bottles into crates. He liked jobs that could be done in the open air, and today the August sun felt pleasingly hot on his shoulders. He heard the deep growl of a lorry's engine and mentally noted that the Tans were moving around a lot this morning.

They had recently moved into Gormanston Camp and already they were making their aggressive presence felt in Balbriggan. Sharing the camp with the Tans were the Auxiliaries – commonly known as the Auxies – a similar mercenary force raised in Britain to bolster the RIC. The Auxies were drawn from the ranks of former officers, but they were as ruthless and brutal as the Tans in their methods, and were already unpopular.

The first Tan had been killed last month, and the Tans and Auxies had let it be known that attacks on their men would be met with violent reprisals. Civilians had been shot and beaten, and homes and businesses wrecked and set ablaze.

Johnny thought that the more the Tans misbehaved the more damage they did to their own cause, and that the mood of the population was increasingly in favour of the rebels. The IRA had stepped up their guerrilla warfare, and the court system had collapsed, with jury trials now suspended. Even in the five and a half weeks that Alice and Stella had been away the conflict had heightened. They would find the Balbriggan that they returned to a changed place, now that the Tans had one of their main bases just outside the town.

Johnny was looking forward to seeing the girls again. Part of it was because he missed their company, but he was also anxious to talk to Alice and find out how she knew about his link to Mr O'Shea. His instincts had stopped him from mentioning her name, however, when giving his reports to the commercial traveller. He had also made sure to say nothing incriminating when he wrote to her in Canada, in case Stella or Commander Radcliffe should see what he wrote. Instead he had sent postcards to both Alice and Stella from places he had visited on day trips during his summer holidays. In return he had received postcards from Toronto, Algonquin Provincial Park, Lake Huron and Niagara Falls.

The girls were currently at sea, but due home next Sunday, and Johnny had found himself counting the days, now that their return was getting near. The biggest thing that had happened in their absence – apart from the Tans moving into Gormanston Camp – was the passing of the Restoration of Order in Ireland Act. This allowed the authorities to replace normal trials with court martials, so that more rebels would be swiftly imprisoned. And coroner's inquests, that could find against Tans and Auxies who had shot people, were now replaced with military courts of enquiry.

But Johnny believed that the power of the state could still be overturned if enough of the population resisted it. Only yesterday he had read how the Ottoman Empire – once far-flung, and powerful – had lost eighty per cent of its territory after ending up on the losing side in the Great War. So if the Ottoman Empire could crumble, surely the British Empire wasn't invincible either.

Johnny finished going through the empty stout bottles. He paused a moment, savouring the morning sunshine before going back inside to see what other jobs Mr Byrne wanted done. Just as he was about to move off he heard the sound of roaring engines approaching at speed, then there was a screech of brakes from the road behind the hotel yard as a truck shuddered to a halt.

Johnny realised that the Mill was being raided. The truck out the back was to make sure nobody escaped through the rear, while the main raiding party would storm in from the front. Johnny ran across the yard and into the kitchen. He saw a frightened looking Mrs Nagle.

'Mother of God, Johnny, what's going on?!'

'It's the Tans,' he said. 'Don't give them lip, and say nothing if they take food or drink.'

'Right.'

Johnny ran on through the kitchen, then along the corridor that led to the lobby. He heard shouting, then on reaching the lobby he saw Mr O'Shea being roughly frogmarched towards the door by a group of heavily armed Tans. Several shocked looking hotel guests were at the reception desk, where Miss Hopkins sat, her face aghast. Mr O'Shea was bleeding from his nose, and Johnny realised that he must have been assaulted and dragged from the dining room. Although Johnny felt scared his instinct was to intervene. Before he could do anything, O'Shea caught his eye and spoke first.

'It's all right, son. It's all right.'

Mr O'Shea always called him by name, and Johnny realised that in addressing him as 'son', he was deliberately giving the impression that they didn't know each other. Following O'Shea's coded lead, Johnny said nothing further as the Tans manhandled the commercial traveller out the door. Johnny crossed the lobby after them and saw them bundling their prisoner into the back of a lorry that had been driven up onto the pavement.

A moment later the engine roared and the Tans drove off. Johnny stood immobile, stunned by the suddenness with which the enemy had struck. O'Shea had said 'it's all right'. Was that code too, meaning that he wouldn't reveal anything about his connection to Johnny. Yes, he thought, it was probably what the quick-thinking O'Shea had been trying to tell him. So the chances were that he was safe enough for now.

But what would happen Mr O'Shea as a prisoner of the Tans? And what would happen if, under torture, he started giving them names?

'Are you all right, Johnny?'

Johnny turned around to see Miss Hopkins, clearly shaken herself, but looking with concern at him.

'Yes,' he lied. 'Yes, I'm OK...'

CHAPTER TWENTY-SIX

Stella stood unmoving at the ship's rail as the Dublin boat eased out into the muddy waters of the Mersey. The Liverpool dockside was busy with craft of every sort, from transatlantic steamers to ferries crossing the river to Birkenhead. Silhouetted against the blue of the sky Stella could see the Liverbirds, symbols of the city, atop one of the finest stone buildings on the Pier Head. But despite the liveliness of the scene, Stella's mind was elsewhere, and she had mixed feelings as they set out on the last leg of their journey back to Ireland from Canada.

The holiday had been memorable, and it had been wonderful to see Mom again and to spend time with her grandfather. Mom had even organised a nurse to look after Granddad for some of their stay so that Stella, her parents, and Alice could travel about Ontario. It had been great having Alice along for company – they had never had a serious disagreement in the whole six weeks – and Stella had enjoyed re-visiting Algonquin Park and Niagara Falls, seeing them afresh through Alice's excited eyes.

Leaving Mom behind had been sad though, and there was no escaping the fact that her tear-filled farewell to Granddad was probably their last goodbye. Granddad was religious, and he seemed resigned to his ailing health, but Stella still found it hard to come to terms with possibly not seeing him again.

She couldn't even wish for the day when Mom would rejoin herself and Dad in Ireland – that would be like wishing Granddad dead. But if the ghost of Granddad seemed to hover in the background, she had at least seen off another ghost. Her fear that Toronto would have too many bad memories had been unfounded, and although she would never forget George, after this trip she felt that she could move on in her life. Once or twice she had wavered, and felt the old guilt beginning to rise. But she had remembered Johnny's advice, and had told herself that just as she would have wanted George to escape the bear, so he too would have wanted her to get away.

'Hey, Stella! You're in another world!' said Alice, breaking her reverie.

Stella turned to her fiend, impressed by Alice's ability to put on a thick Liverpool accent.

'I still can't do a Balbriggan accent,' said Stella. 'And you sound like you were reared at the Pier Head!'

'It's an easy accent to do,' answered Alice.

'That's probably because you're Irish,' said Commander Radcliffe.

Stella looked at her father with curiosity. 'Why would being Irish make an English accent easy?'

'Because Scouse – that's what they call the Liverpool accent – it came from all the Irish who settled in Liverpool. Before that, people here had a Lancashire accent.'

'Really?'

'Yes. And when you mixed the Irish accent with the Lancashire accent, hey presto, Scouse was born.'

'How do you know these things, Dad?' asked Stella.

'Your old dad knows many things!' he answered with a smile.

Just then the ship's engine took on a deeper note, and the vessel began to pick up speed as it moved further out into the river. Stella watched as the enormous warehouses of Liverpool's docklands slipped by.

'Well, next stop, Ireland,' said Alice.

'Yeah,' answered Stella, aware that much had happened in their absence, and wondering what awaited them in Balbriggan. 'Next stop, Ireland…'

The steam train hurtled northwards, trailing a black smokestack that gradually faded into the summer sky. Although the day was warm, the compartment window was closed to keep out smuts from the engine. Alice sat in the window seat, gazing out at the passing countryside without really taking it in. Her mind was on her destination, and she was looking forward to seeing Mam when the train reached Balbriggan station. She was also a little anxious, now that she would be meeting Johnny again.

Both of them had been careful in what they had written to each other, but now they would have to have a proper conversation about Johnny's secret work for O'Shea. On balance, she was glad that she had disobeyed O'Shea's order to say nothing to Johnny. Even if Johnny resented her interference she was hopeful he wouldn't report it to Mr O'Shea. And who could tell, perhaps her warning to be careful had kept Johnny safe, and discouraged him from taking needless risks. If that was the case then it had been worth showing her hand.

Alice's musings were cut short by the sound of loud voices in the corridor outside their compartment. Stella and Commander Radcliffe had been chatting about the recent trip to Algonquin Park but now their conversation trailed off.

Suddenly the sliding door was pulled across and two Auxies brandishing pistols stepped into the compartment. Even though she had done nothing wrong, Alice felt nervous. The Auxies, being former officers, were usually better educated than the Tans, but she knew their behaviour could still be brutal and unpredictable, especially when they had drink taken.

'Spot check,' said the first man. 'Identify yourselves and state your destination!'

Alice thought the two Auxies looked sober, but she was still unsettled by their aggressive demeanour and the deadly looking Webley pistols that they were brandishing.

'Alice Goodman,' she answered a little shakily. 'Travelling to Balbriggan.'

'What for?'

'I live there. My mother owns the Mill Hotel.'

'And you, sir?' asked the second Auxie, with a hint of mockery on the word sir.

Alice thought she saw a flicker of anger on the face of her friend's father, but Commander Radcliffe kept his tone neutral.

'Wing Commander Bernard Radcliffe, Royal Air Force, Baldonnel Station. Travelling to Balbriggan with my daughter, Stella.'

Alice saw that the Auxies were a bit taken aback. 'Not travelling in uniform, sir?'

'Most officers don't, when on holiday with their families,' answered Commander Radcliffe with a slight edge to his voice. 'I think you can be on your way, chaps.'

Alice could see that the Auxies didn't like being dismissed. But the combination of Commander Radcliffe's rank, his educated English accent, and his confidence carried the day.

'Very good, sir,' said the first Auxie, after a slight pause. 'Good day to you.'

'Good day, gentlemen,' answered Commander Radcliffe stiffly.

The Auxies left the compartment, and Alice felt like cheering as they made their retreat. Instead she settled for giving Stella a quick wink, then looked out the window again.

She realised that they were approaching Skerries, after which the next stop would be Balbriggan.

It was hard to believe that it was only six weeks since they had left. Since then she had crossed the Atlantic, gone canoeing on Lake Huron, hiked in the wilderness of Algonquin, and had her photograph taken at the mighty Niagara Falls. And now it was over, leaving her with her memories, and her souvenirs of the trip.

She had spent all of her remaining Canadian dollars on presents, and in her suitcase she had souvenirs for Mam, Johnny, Robert, Mr Tardelli, and several of her school friends.

The train left Skerries station, and after a moment Stella tapped her on the knee. 'Nearly home, Alice. Excited?'

'Yes. But it's been the trip of a lifetime, thank you both so much.'

'Our pleasure, Alice,' said Commander Radcliffe, 'our pleasure.'

'Still nice to be home, though, right?' said Stella.

'Yes, still nice to be home…' answered Alice, even though she knew it was only half true. She was looking forward to seeing Mam, and of course Balbriggan was home. But she would have to deal with Johnny. And maybe even with Mr O'Shea. Canada had been a break from reality, but now she was back to a country at war. And how, she wondered, were they all going to handle that?

CHAPTER TWENTY-SEVEN

Johnny waited restlessly in the woods by the river, hoping that Alice could get away from her mother and meet him during his morning work break. They could have spoken in the Mill, but for the conversation they needed to have it was better to meet secretly.

It was five days now since Mr O'Shea had been arrested, and Johnny had been living on his nerves. He had prayed that O'Shea wouldn't talk, but prisoners could break under torture, and there was no telling what information might be revealed.

More immediately, he needed to know how Alice had found out that he was working for Mr O'Shea, and if she had told anyone else. He hadn't been able to raise it while Alice was in Canada, but now he had to know how much his secret role had been exposed.

Just then he heard a snapping twig, and a moment later there was a rustle in the bushes, and Alice stepped into the sun-dappled clearing.

'I'm glad you made it,' said Johnny.

'Sorry for keeping you. I got out as soon as I could.'

Johnny was looking forward to hearing about Alice's Canadian adventures, but that would have to wait. 'What you said the day you were leaving, Alice. It's been worrying me ever since.'

'Sorry for just blurting it out at the last minute. But I had to, I was afraid something might happen you while I was away.'

'What do you know about me and Mr O'Shea? And *how* do you know?'

Alice looked nervous, then spoke quickly. 'I know you've been spying for him. And I know you're going to be angry with me, Johnny, for interfering. But you're my friend, and I was worried about you. So I asked him to stop putting you in danger.'

'What?'

'I…I searched his room, and found a notebook with stuff about the army and the RIC. And…and a reference to you.'

'To me? My name was in this notebook?'

'Yes.'

'Oh my God. I'm sunk!'

'Why?'

'Haven't you heard?'

'Heard what?'

'Mr O'Shea's been arrested. Did your mother not tell you?'

Johnny could see the shock on Alice's face.

'No,' she said. 'We were so caught up talking about Canada, and all-'

'The Tans took him last Wednesday,' Johnny interrupted. 'If they find that notebook I'm a goner.'

Alice looked thoughtful. 'I warned him about the notebook. So chances are, he hid it somewhere safe.'

'Chances are? Suppose chances aren't?!'

'Five days have passed, Johnny. If they'd found it, they would have come for you by now. He must have hidden it, and not given your name.'

'Not yet.'

'If he's held out for five days you're probably safe. But Johnny, you've got to stop. What you're doing was dangerous before. It's lethal now with Tans and Auxies everywhere. Promise me you'll stop.'

Johnny's mind was racing and he thought back to something that Alice had said earlier. 'You say you went to Mr O'Shea?'

'Yes.'

'Did you tell anyone else?'

'No.'

'So, how did you plan to get him to stop using me?'

Alice looked uncomfortable. 'I…I threatened him with the police.'

'And then he got arrested by the Tans?'

Alice looked at him in horror. 'No, Johnny! No, that's not what happened. I swear I never reported him. It was just a threat. I wanted him to stop putting you at risk. Please, Johnny. you've got to believe me – I never betrayed him.'

Johnny looked at her for a long moment, and he knew instinctively that she was telling the truth. 'OK. OK, I believe you.'

Alice looked relieved. 'In actual fact,' she said, 'he ended up threatening me.'

'How?'

'He pretty much said that Mam and me…our lives would be

in danger if I said anything to anyone. Including talking to you.'

'God', said Johnny. 'I don't believe this…'

'It's all true.'

'And yet you warned me?'

'I had to.'

Johnny didn't know what to say, and Alice reached out and touched his arm.

'Forget Mr O'Shea for now, Johnny. He could be in prison for ages. You've got to think about yourself. It's much too dangerous what you're doing. Please, promise that you'll stop.'

Johnny knew that Alice was right about the increased danger. He thought for a moment, then turned to her.

'I don't know how Mr O'Shea got caught. I don't know if he was betrayed or if he slipped up himself. I don't know what's going on, Alice. So I'm sorry. But until I do know – I can't promise anything.'

CHAPTER TWENTY-EIGHT

'Remember, girls, the three most important things in music,' said Mr Tardelli.

'Practice, practice, practice!' cried Stella and Alice in unison.

Mr Tardelli smiled as the girls laughingly waved farewell and left the classroom.

Most pupils were pleased to get out of school once normal hours ended, but Stella was happy to attend the private music lessons that Mr Tardelli gave each Monday night in one of the classrooms.

She was in her third week of secondary school but she had quickly adapted to the new regime, and felt at home now as they walked down the corridor leading to the school yard.

They stepped out into the September evening, the air a little chilly as a quarter moon rose in the sky.

'I wish school music class could be like tonight's lesson,' said Alice.

'Yeah, "For Me and My Gal" is a great tune. I love the way the melody kind of jumps around.

'Me too,' said Alice. 'But can you picture Sister Mary Joseph singing that?'

Stella laughed. '"Soul of My Saviour" is more her style.'

Alice imitated the nun, joining her hands in mock piety, and

Stella laughed again as they made for home in the darkening night.

They lapsed into a companionable silence, and Stella found herself reflecting on how much had happened in the month since they had returned from Canada. Women in America had got the vote, a new country called Lebanon had come into existence, and a record had been set when a motor cyclist had managed to travel at one hundred miles per hour. It seemed like everything in the world was speeding up, and change was coming at an ever-faster pace.

In India, Mr Ghandi was calling for non-co-operation with British rule, and despite her father's belief in the Empire, Stella wondered if British rule could continue as before. Certainly here in Ireland the Tans and the Auxies had alienated much of the population, and Stella sensed that even Dad was ashamed of how they behaved in the name of the Crown.

'Penny for your thoughts!' said Alice.

'Just…just thinking what the future holds.'

'Well, as Mr Tardelli would say, "the future is an open book".'

'That's the problem though, isn't it?' said Stella. 'It could be something great. Or something awful. And right now, I haven't a clue which it will be…'

'Let me be blunt, son. Your time is up in Balbriggan.'

Johnny could hardly believe his ears. Dusk had fallen and he was in a darkened corner in the backyard of the Mill. He was talking to a squat, tough looking man with a Belfast accent who called himself Smith. Smith – if that was really his name – had shown up unannounced, introduced himself as an associate of Mr O'Shea, and told Johnny that they needed to speak somewhere private.

Johnny had felt a bit abandoned when no-one from the IRA had contacted him following the arrest of O'Shea. And now, suddenly, contact had been made and Smith was telling him that he should flee the Mill.

'Why would I want to leave Balbriggan?' asked Johnny.

'It's not what you want, son. We're pawns in a bigger game. And these are your orders.'

'Orders? I didn't get any orders when I was worried sick after Mr O'Shea was arrested. I didn't get any contact.'

'And why do you think that was?'

'I don't know,' said Johnny. 'You tell me.'

'Because they'd be watching to see if anything happened after O'Shea was lifted. Any flurry of activity. Anyone suddenly quitting his job and leaving. That's why we waited till now, for your sake as well as everyone else's.'

'And supposing he'd talked? Given them my name? I'd have been here, a sitting duck for them to arrest.'

'He was never going to talk.'

'Easy for you to say.'

'I know Oliver O'Shea. You were never in danger from him talking.'

'So where is he now?'

'In prison for the moment.'

'For the moment?'

'We've plans to address that. But I can't discuss the details. What I can say is this. You've done really well, Johnny. O'Shea speaks highly of you. And it's been noted by people higher up. Very high up.'

'Then let me stay here and keep going. I've a job here, my friends are here. I don't want to leave.'

'We can get you a job somewhere else. You can see your friends again when all this is over. Right now, though, we've another mission for you.'

'Supposing I don't want another mission?'

'Would it make a difference if I told you Michael Collins himself requested this?'

Johnny was completely taken aback. Michael Collins was his hero, the legendary leader of the rebels, and the man masterminding the guerrilla warfare against the British.

'Here's the deal, Johnny,' said Smith, his tone more persuasive now. 'You don't have to take this mission. There's risk involved, and you're a young lad, and we don't want to force you. You've already served your country, and if you feel you've done enough, so be it. Either way though, you leave Balbriggan. For security reasons, it's been decided to pull you out – and that's a direct order. Understood?'

Johnny was struggling to take in all that had been said. But he knew that even in an underground army a direct order had to be obeyed. 'Understood,' he said reluctantly.

'Good,' said Smith. 'So, if you're leaving Balbriggan anyway, do you want to stay part of the fight for freedom?'

Johnny paused, still disappointed to be ordered to leave his friends and his job. But in truth as soon as he had heard the words Michael Collins he knew that he would take the mission, whatever it was. 'Yes, I want to stay part of it.'

'Good lad.'

'So, what's this mission?'

'Not unlike what you've been doing. Gathering information. But in a…a higher value place. It needs to be set up, but you'll be given the full details when the time is right.'

'So, when do I leave Balbriggan?'

'Tomorrow.'

'Tomorrow?! I can't just walk out of my job and leave them high and dry.'

Smith shook his head, smiling disbelievingly. 'There's a war on, Johnny. The Mill Hotel being without a boots – that's small potatoes.'

'What am I supposed to tell them?'

'That you've got another job.'

'Where?'

'Well away from here. In Limerick. Or Cork. Wherever you like. Keep it vague.'

'And how am I supposed to have got this job?'

'Somebody staying here thought you were a good worker and offered you a post. But don't feel you owe them a detailed explanation. Like I say, keep things vague.'

'And where am I really going?'

'Thurles, in county Tipperary. You can lie low there for a while till we fix things up. Think of it as a bit of a break.'

'Are you coming with me?'

'No, I'm going to Belfast on the next train tonight. All the stuff you need is with a sympathiser here in town. Train tickets, directions, spending money, he'll give it all to you.'

'Why didn't you just give it to me yourself?'

'Too many spot checks. If I'm stopped, I don't want to have to spin a story about why a Belfast man has train tickets and directions to Tipperary. Do you know Clonard Street?'

'Yes, I play football there.'

'Know Mr Clifford's house?'

'Mr Clifford is my contact?'

'Yes.'

'I never even knew he was a republican.'

'Until tonight, he didn't know you were either. More secure for everyone that way. Never underestimate the importance of secrecy.'

'You've thought of everything, haven't you?' said Johnny.

'Not everything, son. But as much as we can to keep our people safe. Thanks for all you've done. And good luck in the future.' He offered Johnny his hand and shook firmly. 'God save Ireland.'

'God save Ireland,' answered Johnny, then he stood unmoving in the yard, his head swimming as Smith disappeared into the shadows.

Two bangs rang out in the evening air, and Alice stopped dead. She was halfway back to the Mill after her music lesson with Stella, but now she turned to her friend. 'God, Stella! That sounded like shots.'

Stella looked concerned. 'Yeah, it did.'

'Let's check it out!'

'Should we? Maybe the smart thing is to get home.'

Alice knew this was what her mother would say too. Tonight, though, Mam was on an overnight visit to a friend in Wexford, so for once Alice was her own boss, and she decided to make the most of it.

'It sounded like it came from the direction we're headed,' she said. 'We could have a quick look on the way.' Alice sensed that Stella was probably just as curious as she was and she looked at her appealingly. 'Come on, you'll never get to sleep wondering what happened. Let's find out!'

'OK.'

The two girls picked up their pace, then Alice saw that up ahead a crowd had gathered. She reasoned that whatever danger had existed must be over now, as more people hurried to see what had happened.

They reached the edge of the crowd and Alice recognised Mr Sweeney, who ran a small grocer's shop, and who always seemed to know what was going on in the town.

'What's happening, Mr Sweeney?' she asked.

The grocer turned to her, his expression grim. 'I wouldn't go any closer, Alice,' he said. 'Two RIC men have been shot.'

'Are they…are they all right?' asked Stella.

'No love, they're not. Lord have mercy on them, but they're both dead.'

Alice swallowed hard, shocked that the war had come so close to home.

'Who killed them?' said Stella.

'No-one knows. They came out of the pub and shots were fired from the dark.'

'This…this is going to mean big trouble,' said Alice.

'Worse than you can imagine,' said Mr Sweeney. 'The men they shot are the Burke Brothers. One of them had just been promoted to District Inspector. Know what his job was?'

Alice shook her head. 'No, what?'

'Training Auxies. When they hear about this there'll be hell to pay.'

'What do you think they'll do?' asked Stella.

'Honest answer, love? Run amok. This will be a bad night in Balbriggan. You'd be well advised to get home and lock your doors.'

All of a sudden Alice wasn't so pleased that Mam was away for the night, and she looked at Stella.

'We should do that,' suggested Stella.

'Yeah,' said Alice. 'Let's go.'

Johnny carefully packed his possessions. He had been given a small, cheap suitcase when leaving the orphanage, and now it lay open on his bed as he filled it with his limited collection of clothes. He grappled with a whirl of emotions, one moment sad to leave, the next moment excited by the thought of an important mission. He was still fearful for Mr O'Shea, but flattered that his handler had recommended him to no less a figure than Michael Collins.

His thoughts were disturbed by a knock on his bedroom door. Johnny rarely had visitors to his room, and he stopped what he was doing. 'Who's that?' he called out.

'Alice.'

Johnny crossed to the door and opened it. To his surprise, Stella was also there. 'What's…what's up?' said Johnny.

'There's been a shooting,' answered Alice. 'Did you not hear it?'

'No, I've been indoors.'

'Can we step in, we need to talk?'

'Yeah, come in,' said Johnny ushering the two girls into the bedroom.

'We thought we should warn you,' explained Alice.

'Warn me?'

'Two RIC men have been killed,' said Stella. 'Shot dead outside Smiths pub. One of them was linked to the Auxies.'

'When the Auxies and the Tans find out, there'll be murder,' said Alice. 'Balbriggan's going to pay for this.'

Johnny was about to respond, but Stella indicated the suitcase on the bed.

'Are you going somewhere?'

Johnny wasn't sure how to explain and he nodded uncertainly. 'I'm…I'm leaving tomorrow.'

'What?!'

'I've…I've got another job – down the country.'

Alice looked dumbfounded. 'Does…does Mam know this?'

'No. I only found out.'

'Were you just going to leave? Without saying goodbye?'

'Of course not. I wouldn't dream of doing that.'

'Then what's going on, Johnny? When did this all happen?'

Johnny looked at their worried faces and felt guilty. To hell with Mr Smith and his secrecy, he thought. These were his friends. They were entitled to some answers. At the same time Stella was the daughter of an officer, so he had to tread carefully.

'Before I answer your questions, let me ask something, Alice. You said you came to warn me. Have you told Stella what's behind that?'

'I told her the Tans could run riot. That we need to be ready for that.'

'And that's all?'

'Yes.'

'Why, what else is there?' asked Stella.

Johnny hesitated. It was a huge step to reveal what he had been doing. But Stella had trusted him with *her* biggest secret when she had told him about how her brother had died. He had to be honest with her in return. He paused briefly, then looked her in the eye. 'You know I'm a nationalist, Stella. What you don't know is that I've been working for the rebels.'

'Working how?'

'Gathering information.'

'Spying?'

'If you want to call it that. But don't expect me to apologise. The Tans and the Auxies are thugs. You saw them in Bray, you know what they're like. And this is my country, not theirs.'

'So you've what – listened to conversations? Passed on what you've picked up here in the Mill?'

'I've been fighting a secret war for a better Ireland. So yes, that's what I've done.'

'Does that include spying on my dad?'

'I really like your father, Stella. I'd never do anything to harm him. But information about Gormanston Camp or stuff like that – yes, I passed that on. It was my duty.'

Johnny could see that Stella was shocked, and he wondered if he had said too much. 'Are you…are you going to report me to your father?' he asked.

Stella looked at him challengingly. 'What do you take me for?'

'I hope, still your friend. But…'

'But what?'

'But you're also the daughter of a British officer.'

'Yes,' said Stella, 'I am. And I don't apologise for that.' She paused, then continued in a subdued voice. 'I won't be reporting you. I…I couldn't.'

Alice spoke up for the first time. 'So…where does that leave us?'

'I don't know,' said Stella.

'Well, can we all still be friends?' persisted Alice.

Johnny looked at Stella, trying to gain a clue from her expression, and hoping that his spying hadn't ruined everything between them.

She looked serious, but then she nodded. 'I want us to stay friends, no matter what.'

Johnny was touched. 'I'm really glad,' he said. 'If I live to be one hundred, I'll still think of you and Alice as the best friends I've ever had.'

To Johnny's surprise he saw tears welling up in Stella's eyes. She seemed to struggle to find the right words and in the end she just quietly said 'Thank you.'

'Yes, thanks, Johnny,' said Alice. 'And there's loads more we want to hear about your plans. But first things first. The Tans and the Auxies will want revenge, so tonight could be pretty bad. Why don't the three of us face it together? What do you say.'

Johnny looked at the girls, then nodded. 'Yeah,' he said, 'yeah, let's do that.'

Stella felt uncomfortable as she sat behind the desk in Mrs Goodman's office. This was Alice's mother's domain, and it was almost as though she were a trespasser. But Stella knew what she had to do and she reached across the desk and lifted the receiver of the telephone.

Her emotions were still in turmoil after Johnny's dramatic revelation a few minutes earlier. She wished that her father and Johnny weren't on opposite sides; that the Tans and Auxies had never come to Ireland; that life could just be normal. But even as she entertained the thoughts she knew it was pointless. A war was raging, and everyone had to choose sides. Her musings were suddenly interrupted by the operator coming on the line.

'Hello, who do you wish to contact?'

'Wing Commander Radcliffe, please, RAF Baldonnel.'

'One moment, caller.'

'Thank you.'

Stella's thoughts went back to Johnny. It was deeply unfair that he had lived most of his life in a cruel and brutal environment, and she could understand his desire for revolution. But spying for the rebels was an outright act of war, and she wished that he had stayed out of the conflict.

'I'm sorry, caller, but I can't get through to that number.'

'Really? What's the problem?'

'The line is completely dead.'

'Are you getting through to other numbers?'

'Yes, I am. But sometimes the rebels cut the lines to military bases. I'd say that's what's happened to Baldonnel.'

'How long does it normally take to get them working again?'

'It could be hours. It could be tomorrow morning.'

Stella felt her heart sinking.

'I'm sorry, caller.'

'That's all right. Thank you for trying.'

Stella hung up. She had hoped that she could get Dad to travel from Baldonnel to Balbriggan. If he were with them in the Mill they would all be much safer when the Tans descended on the town. But Dad probably had his own problems if there was trouble at Baldonnel. She loved him dearly and hoped that he would be all right. Yet despite her upbringing, and Dad's role as a British officer, there was no denying that her sympathies had shifted.

Huge numbers of Irish people had voted for pro-independence candidates in the most recent election, and Stella felt that in a democracy their wishes couldn't be ignored. And although the Tans and Auxies were supposed to have bolstered the rule of law, in fact their behaviour had turned even more people against British rule.

Meanwhile she and her friends had to get through tonight. And with Dad out of contact they were on their own. She pushed her chair back, and made determinedly for the door.

Alice reckoned this was the calm before the storm. Mr Sweeney had seemed sure that the Tans and Auxies would wreak havoc on Balbriggan, and Alice was dreading their arrival.

She sat on the edge of her bed and opened her savings box. She had graduated from a piggy bank to an ornate wooden box that could be locked, and now she spilled the contents onto the bed. There were pennies, sixpences, shillings, half-crowns, and three one-pound notes. She took up one of the pound notes and wondered how best to give it to Johnny.

She knew that Mam didn't pay him very well and she suspected that his new job in Limerick wouldn't pay a fortune either. Knowing Johnny, she imagined that he'd be too proud to take help, so the best thing would probably be to put the note in an envelope and slip it into his jacket pocket.

It was a big chunk of her savings, but Johnny was a good friend who had had very few breaks in life. Having a little extra money might help him get established in Limerick, and Alice knew she would feel better for knowing he wouldn't go short.

She was still worried about him, however. Since returning from Canada she had asked him several times if he was still passing on information. Johnny had insisted that there had been no contact from the IRA after the arrest of Mr O'Shea, and Alice had believed him. But might he get involved once more down in Limerick? She hoped not, and had encouraged him not to put himself at risk again. Yet part of her couldn't help but admire his bravery, and his willingness to take a stand for what he believed in.

He hadn't given a definite answer about getting involved again, and she sensed that there was no point forcing the issue. She knew that there were people who were prepared to fight bravely to better their lives. Sometimes they were in trade unions and sometimes they were in rebel movements. But what made her admire Johnny was that he didn't just want to better his own life. He wanted a fairer world for everyone, and he was prepared to back his words with action. Alice still hoped that he wouldn't get drawn in again with the rebels. But if he did, she knew he would be doing it for a noble reason.

She thought about it for a moment. Then on impulse she reached out and took a second pound note, rose from the bed and slipped both notes into an envelope.

Johnny felt the knife bite into the potato, then he expertly removed the skin and dropped the peeled potato into a large cauldron of cold water.

'Johnny? What on earth are you at?!' said Stella as she came into the Mill's kitchen.

'I was supposed to have these done for tomorrow,' answered

Johnny. 'I won't have Mrs Goodman saying I slacked off on my last day.'

'Do you care that much what she thinks?'

Johnny shrugged. 'Maybe I shouldn't. But I'm not working out my notice, so I thought I'd at least make sure my chores were done.'

'And are you finished packing?'

'Yeah, except for my clarinet.'

'Where's that?'

'In the band hall. Mr Tardelli was going to have it repaired for me. I'll pick it up and get it repaired myself.' There was no need to reveal that he would first collect his train ticket in Clonard Road, thought Johnny. It was one thing to come clean about himself, but Mr Clifford was entitled to stay under cover.

'Will there be someone in the hall?' asked Stella.

'Even if there's not, the key is always left under the stone outside. I'll go up when I'm finished here.'

'Are you crazy, Johnny? The Tans could arrive at any time.'

'They'll hardly come this soon.'

'They might. Look, forget the potatoes – I'll finish those for you. Just get your clarinet and get back here safely. All right?'

Johnny looked at her, then lowered the knife. 'OK,' he said. 'OK.'

Alice got her nerve up, then rounded the corner into the lobby to meet the assembled staff. She had told Miss Hopkins to gather them, and now Mikey Power, Mr Byrne, and Miss Hopkins herself were waiting for her. The cook, Mrs Nagle, and the rest of the serving staff and maids had all gone home by this hour, and Alice was glad that it was a fairly small group for which she would be responsible.

In Mam's absence, someone needed to take charge, and Alice had decided that it had to be her. Although much younger than any of the others, she was, after all, the owner's daughter, and one day she would be running the Mill. The expected arrival of the Tans had simply brought that day forward, she told herself. The staff were used to taking instructions, so the important thing now was to sound confident and in command.

'Thanks for gathering,' she said, 'I won't keep you long. But we need a plan for when the Tans come.'

'Do you really think they're coming here?' asked Miss Hopkins nervously.

'I'm hoping the Mill won't be top of their list. But they're going to hit Balbriggan after what's happened. We don't know how bad the reprisals will be, but we need to be prepared.'

Hope for the best, prepare for the worst, was Mam's motto. Alice could see, however, that the others were already nervous, so she tried to sound upbeat. 'Maybe they won't come near us, but it's better to be ready. So what we're going to do is lock all the doors.'

'What about the people who are drinking in the bar?' asked Mr Byrne.

'We don't ask them to leave,' answered Alice. 'Let's keep things normal for as long as we can. But we lock the doors and don't let anyone else in. Then when the people in the bar are leaving, Mikey unlocks the door to let them out.'

'What do I do if the Tans tell me to open up?' asked Mikey. 'They're demons when they've drink on them.'

'Let's see what they're like when they get here. If we can persuade them that we're closed, that would be best. But if they're in a rage we don't argue. And if they do get in, don't cross them. All right?'

The others nervously agreed.

'OK,' said Alice, 'you can go back to the bar, Mr Byrne. Miss Hopkins, you man reception, please. And Mikey, the only people you let in are any residents who went out. Or Johnny Dunne – he should be back shortly.'

'Where's Johnny gone at this hour?'

'He went to get his clarinet. All right, that's it,' said Alice, trying to sound confident. 'We get on with things and hope for the best.'

'Mother of God, they're gone mad!' Mr Clifford shook his head in disbelief as he and Johnny stood outside his cottage in Clonard Street. Sheets of flame were leaping into the night sky from thatched cottage roofs that had been set on fire further down the road.

Johnny had collected his train ticket and directions for Thurles, but had felt obliged to stay a bit longer and help the older man to barricade the cottage against the expected arrival of the Tans at Clonard Street. This area was known to be the main republican stronghold in Balbriggan, and Mr Clifford expected the Tans would make it a priority in reprisals for the earlier shooting.

He hadn't been wrong, and lorries full of outraged Tans and Auxies had roared into town hell-bent on vengeance. Within minutes they had poured petrol onto the thatched roofs in Clonard Street and set them alight. The rest of the town was being targeted too, and Johnny could hear windows being smashed and people screaming as the Tans ran amok. Other buildings were already alight, and Johnny saw that the pub at the bottom of the road was burning furiously.

Johnny realised that the barricading they had done to Mr Clifford's cottage was useless against fire. In fact, if Mr Clifford was barricaded in and the Tans torched the roof, he could be burnt to death.

'I think we wasted our time barricading,' said Johnny.

'I thought they might break in,' answered Mr Clifford. 'I wasn't expecting petrol.'

Johnny looked at him sympathetically. He was a trim seventy-year-old, but Johnny feared that his age wouldn't guarantee his safety with the Tans and Auxies on the rampage.

'Buckets of water and wet blankets are your best hope now,' said Johnny. 'I'll give you a hand.'

'Better you get back to the Mill, son.'

Johnny was about to object, but Mr Clifford held up his hand, cutting him off. 'You're a brave lad, Johnny, and I appreciate the offer. But we don't want anyone making a link between us.'

With all the chaos that was unfolding, Johnny hadn't thought about that.

'And don't worry, I'll survive. Now you get back safely to the Mill.' He offered Johnny his hand. 'Good luck wherever they send you next.'

Johnny hesitated briefly, then shook hands. 'Thanks, Mr Clifford.'

'God save Ireland!'

'God save Ireland!'

Johnny gave him a wave, then started down the street. *But the Mill would have to wait. First he had to get his clarinet.* He had said nothing about it to the older man – he didn't expect anyone else to understand the instrument's importance – but he couldn't leave without it. He heard screaming and more windows being broken as he headed for Bridge Street. He crossed to the opposite footpath to avoid a group of Auxies who were roughing up two local men. Already he could feel the heat from the blazing roofs and he dodged around families who were fleeing their burning homes.

In making for the band hall, he would be going into the heart of all the trouble, and he paused a moment, gathering his nerve. Then he steeled himself and strode forward, heading into the chaos.

Alice tried to keep her voice from wavering. The violence and destruction the Tans had unleashed was far worse than she had expected, and from the windows of the Mill she had seen multiple buildings blazing. Johnny hadn't returned yet, which was also worrying. But she had to appear calm for the staff gathered in the lobby – she could already see that Miss Hopkins was close to breaking. Mr Byrne and Mikey Power were holding up, but Alice sensed that they were nervous too.

'OK,' she said, 'it's worse than we thought, but we needn't panic. The good thing is, all our bar customers have left. And we've asked our guests to say in their rooms, and they've all agreed.'

'What will happen us when the Tans come here?' said Miss Hopkins. 'They've no respect for women, I've heard stories…'

'It's all right, Miss Hopkins, you won't have to deal with them. And, Mr Byrne, as barman I know you normally decide who gets served, and you have to account for stock. Not tonight. If they demand to be served, serve them. If they take drink and don't pay for it, let them have it. You won't be held responsible, so don't put yourself at risk for the sake of a few bob. OK?'

'OK. Thanks.'

'The same goes for you, Mikey. If they take sandwiches or food from the kitchen, don't be a hero. Just let them do it. Understood?'

'Understood.'

'And what about me?' said Miss Hopkins.

'You'll be safe in our family quarters,' said Alice. She turned to

Mikey and Mr Byrne. 'If it's all right with you, I think it's better to have men on duty if we're serving drunken Tans.'

'Absolutely,' said Mikey. 'They can be awful blackguards with women.'

'So if it gets messy, myself, Stella and Miss Hopkins will lock ourselves into our family quarters – Stella is there already. Is that all right with you, Mr Byrne?'

'Completely.'

'And any Tans or Auxies we're dealing with, play up the fact that the Mill has always welcomed Crown Forces. OK?'

Mikey and Mr Byrne nodded in agreement.

'Right,' said Alice. 'Fingers crossed, it mightn't be too bad. But anyone who's good at praying, this would be a good time to pray.'

Johnny turned into Bridge Street. The heat from the burning public house was overwhelming, and he had to shield his face from the blaze. He heard the sound of a roaring engine, then saw another lorry screech to a halt further up the street. Uniformed men jumped out the back of the vehicle, and it seemed to Johnny that every Tan and Auxie from Gormanston Camp must be descending on Balbriggan. He swallowed hard, trying to keep his fear under control. Supposing they stopped him and searched him? How would he explain the train ticket to Thurles?

No, he thought, tonight the Tans weren't interested in asking questions. Tonight they were out for revenge. It was reassuring in one way, in that they were unlikely to discover that he was a spy. But it was terrifying too, in that these men were out of control; and drunken Tans and Auxies were capable of anything.

Come on, he told himself. *Just get to the band hall, pick up the clarinet and get back to the Mill in one piece.*

He crossed the road and was about to turn into George's Hill. Instead he came to a sudden stop. Blocking his way was a Tan. Silhouetted against a burning building, he looked like a figure from a nightmare. But he was frighteningly real, and he quickly raised his hand, aiming a Webley revolver at Johnny's chest.

'Something's happened,' said Stella. 'Johnny should be back by now.'

'I know,' said Alice. 'I hope to God he's all right.'

They had been putting a good face on things for the sake of the nervous Miss Hopkins, but now the receptionist had left the Goodman's living room to use the toilet, and they could speak freely.

Stella rose from the table. 'There's only one thing for it,' she said.

'What?'

'I'm going to go after him.'

'No, Stella!'

'I have to. I felt guilty for years over George. That's not happening to me again.'

'This is completely different.'

'No, Alice, it's someone I care about who's in danger. I'm not standing idly by.'

'But what can you do?'

'What I did that day in Bray. Play the part of a British officer's daughter.'

'That was in broad daylight, with lots of witnesses, and just a few Tans.'

'So what?'

'There's chaos tonight. Anything could happen and there'd be no witnesses. Supposing they don't care who you are? Supposing…supposing that instead of finding Johnny, you find yourself being attacked?'

Zig-zagging to make himself harder to shoot, Johnny ran through the burning streets of Balbriggan.

He had talked his way past the Black and Tan with the Webley pistol, then a second Tan had drunkenly challenged him. Johnny had already been running, the air reverberating with screams, shouts and the sound of smashing glass, and he had taken a chance and refused to stop. Shouting out that he was making for his granny's house, he had sprinted past the surprised Tan.

Now he crouched low as he ran, wanting to make himself a

smaller target in case the man shot at him. Panting for breath, he rounded a corner, out of the man's line of fire. He kept running, in case the Tan followed him. No shot was fired, however, and after a moment he slowed down. He felt exhilarated to have got the better of both Tans, then he turned the next corner.

His satisfaction at outwitting his enemies quickly died when he saw that the band hall was on fire. It wasn't blazing as uncontrollably as the cottages on Clonard Street, but the building was burning and his clarinet was at risk. His chest was still heaving from sprinting, but he forced himself to run again and sped in the direction of the hall.

* * *

'Please, Stella,' said Alice appealingly. 'Don't go out, it's much too dangerous.' She could see from her friend's face that she hadn't swayed her and she tried a different tack. 'I'll get the blame if anything happens to you. Mam will kill me.'

'She won't, because nothing's going to happen me.'

'You don't know that, Stella.'

'I know what I have to do.'

'You haven't really thought this through.'

'I have, Alice. I'm going to find Johnny because he's a true-blue friend. But I'm also doing it for myself.'

'You don't have to prove anything, Stella. Not to me, or Johnny, or even yourself.'

'Maybe not. Or then again, maybe I do. Either way, I'm going to find Johnny. Don't try to stop me, Alice, just wish me luck. Please?'

Alice looked at her friend and realised that there was no persuading her. 'OK,' she said, reaching out and squeezing her arm. 'Good luck, Stella. I'll be praying for both of you.'

Johnny climbed the wall at the rear of the band hall. He could feel the heat from the burning building, but to his relief there were no Tans or Auxies in the back yard. He dropped down from the wall, then ran towards the rear door.

Smoke was escaping from a smashed window on the second floor of the building and he knew that he needed to move quickly. He bent down and reached under the potted plant at the door. To his horror, there was no sign of the key. He got down on his knees and felt along the ground. This time his hand closed on the metal of the key ring, and he experienced a surge of relief.

He rose swiftly, inserted the key and turned it in the lock.

Stella felt scared, now that the moment of truth had come. But there was no going back, and she nodded to Mikey Power to unlock the door of the Mill and let her out. As a precaution, she had nipped into the hotel kitchen and armed herself, in case the worst came to the worst.

Outside the night sky was lit up with flames from burning buildings, and the autumn air carried the acrid smell of smoke.

'I hope you know what you're doing!' said Mikey dubiously.

'I do. It'll be fine, Mikey.'

But *did* she know what she was doing? Her plan was to make for the band hall at speed, yet at the same time to take a route that avoided, as much as possible, the worst of the burning and looting. But supposing Johnny wasn't there? Or he was under arrest? Or worse still, injured?

Stella tried to still her racing mind. *Concentrate on one thing at a time,* she told herself. *Get to the band hall, and play everything else by ear.*

'Thanks, Mikey,' she said, stepping out onto the pavement

'Good luck, Miss.'

Stella nodded in acknowledgement, then turned away and set off into the night.

Johnny breathed in through the handkerchief that he wore as a mask. His eyes smarted from the smoke in the band room and the heat was overpowering. But he had found the clarinet in the press where Mr Tardelli had left it, and that made all the risks that he had taken seem worthwhile.

The rafters were burning steadily now, and Johnny turned to

make for the door. Suddenly there was a loud crack and the ceiling began to collapse. He tried not to panic, but masonry began to fall down. Johnny raised his hands to try to protect himself, but it was too late. A heavy piece of masonry hit him on the head, and he fell to the floor as the rest of the ceiling collapsed into the room.

Alice gripped the telephone tightly as she sat at the desk in her mother's office. 'I need the fire brigade, Operator, it's urgent!'

'Where are you calling from?'

'The Mill Hotel in Balbriggan.'

'Is the Mill on fire?'

'No but half of Balbriggan is!'

'I've already been onto the fire service for other callers. They know about the fires in Balbriggan.'

'Then where are they?!' demanded Alice. 'I looked over the town from our top window – it's an inferno!'

'Like I say, they've been notified.'

'Can I speak to whoever is in charge of the fire brigade?'

The operator hesitated. 'I can put you through, love, but…'

'But what?'

'This is…this is off the record, all right?'

'Right.'

'The story we're hearing is that drunken Tans and Auxies are running riot, that they're the ones setting the fires. If armed policemen are setting the town alight, what can the fire brigade do?'

Alice was about to protest, when Mr Byrne burst into the office.

'The Tans have arrived! A lorry load of them pulled up outside!'

Alice felt her stomach tightening in fear but she tried to sound calm. 'All right, Operator, thanks for your help,' she said, hanging up. Then she rose quickly from the desk. 'Right, let's face them.'

Johnny lay on the floor. His arms and legs ached from being hit by the collapsing roof. His head throbbed too from where the heavy masonry had struck him, and his throat hurt from breathing in the smoke.

He reached up and touched the top of his head. To his relief, he found that he wasn't bleeding and he realised that his thick mop of hair had cushioned the blow somewhat. The other good news was that his clarinet was in its case on the ground beside him. *Time to get out of here.*

He went to get up but found that his right foot was trapped in rubble that was under a fallen beam. He tried to wriggle free, but to his horror found himself trapped. He felt a tremor of panic, but forced himself not to give in to it. Seeing things clearly could be the difference between life and death, and he made himself think logically.

His leg was sore but not broken – he knew he would never have been able to wriggle it if it were broken. Presumably the beam hadn't fallen directly on his leg, but must have rolled onto the rubble under which his foot was trapped. So if he could free himself he would be able to escape from the burning building.

He sat up and reached forward. If he could lift the beam even a little it might free his foot. He slipped his fingers under the beam and pushed hard. The beam didn't move. He tried again, using all of his strength, but the beam only shifted fractionally. Sweat trickled down his face, and the smoke was making him cough. But he ignored his discomfort and the worsening fire. Instead he concentrated again on moving the beam, knowing that his life lay in the balance.

Stella sped down the steep incline of High Street as a steam train thundered across the viaduct spanning the Bracken River. She wondered what the train passengers must think, with buildings all over Balbriggan blazing furiously, then she dismissed the thought. Her plan was to cross the river down near the harbour, and so avoid the main street on her way to the band hall.

Shouts, curses and screams rent the night air, and the horrible crackling sound of burning timber emanated from blazing buildings. Stella tried to block out all the noise and instead kept a sharp lookout for any sign of Johnny as she crossed the river and drew nearer to her destination.

She turned a corner, only to run straight into the path of a

Black and Tan. The man had a rifle in one hand and a bottle of whiskey in the other. He lowered the bottle from his mouth and pointed the rifle one-handedly at Stella.

'Where do you think you're going?!' he demanded.

'I'm looking for a friend of mine. I'm afraid something might have happened to him.'

'Why? Little Shinner, is he?'

'No, absolutely not!' answered Stella immediately. In truth, that was exactly what Johnny was, but she needed to stay on the right side of the Tan, and the lie had come automatically.

'Then he ain't got nothing to fear, has he?' said the man, his speech slightly slurred.

Despite the seriousness of the situation a tiny part of Stella wanted to correct his grammar. But this wasn't the moment to worry about a double negative. More importantly, she didn't want to waste valuable time. 'I just want to find my friend and make sure he's all right.'

'That so?'

Time to play the officer card. 'My father is a Wing Commander in the RAF.'

'Really?'

'Yes.'

'Bully for him. Must be nice to be a *Wing Commander*,' he added sarcastically before taking a slug from the whiskey bottle. 'But here's my question for the *Wing Commander*,' said the man, suddenly looking Stella in the eye. 'What the hell is he doing letting you out in this lot?'

'He's not here tonight, but I assure you–'

'*You assure me,*' mimicked the Tan. 'It ain't your place to assure me, Little-Miss-High-and-Mighty. Now get yourself home.'

'Look, I really need to–'

'Get yourself home before I tan your hide!' said the man drawing close.

Stella saw that reasoning wasn't going to work. Desperate measures were required, and she got up her nerve, then bowed her head as though cowed. She slipped her hand into her pocket, glad now that she had had the foresight to arm herself in the Mill's kitchen. While the Tan thought she was defeated she suddenly pulled her hand out and threw a fistful of pepper right into his eyes. The man cried out in fury as the pepper blinded him, and Stella rounded him and sprinted down the road.

The man screamed an oath and fired his rifle. Stella felt as though what happened next took place in slow motion. She heard the sound of the shot, the bullet ricocheted off the ground near her feet, then went through the window pane of a shop, shattering the glass.

Stella sprinted on without looking round, fearful that at any moment another bullet might hit her in the back. Instead she reached the next corner, rounded it at speed, and continued on her way to the band hall.

Johnny coughed painfully as the smoke stung his lungs. Despite all his efforts he hadn't been able to lift the beam enough to free his foot. The smoke had thickened, and he was getting woozy from lack of oxygen. The effort to free his leg had been exhausting, and part of him wanted to stop struggling and simply rest. It would be so much easier to close his eyes. Yet even as he thought it, Johnny knew that to lie back now would be fatal. Just then he was hit by another fit of coughing. Ignoring the wracking pain in his chest, he forced himself to grab the beam and push again. He heaved with every last ounce of his strength and felt the beam shift a little. Before he could move his foot, however, he breathed in more smoke and fell back, coughing uncontrollably. The woozy feeling suddenly worsened, and he felt his strength ebbing away as he slipped into unconsciousness.

'No need for any problems, Gentlemen!' said Alice, drawing herself up to her full height and trying to sound confident. 'The Mill has always welcomed Crown forces!'

'We'll do as we like,' shouted a drunken Tan, 'welcome or no welcome!'

Alice realised that the Tans milling about the lobby and shouting for drink were in the mood for trouble, and that she would have to tread carefully. About ten of then had demanded entry to the Mill, and Mikey Power had followed her orders and allowed them in. It was obvious that they already had drink taken, and they were angry and heavily armed – a dangerous combination.

She had learnt from watching her mother how to handle people who were drunk or disorderly. Mam's technique was to act as though she was confident that the person involved would do the right thing and stop misbehaving. It often worked for her mother, and Alice decided to try it now with the Tans.

'You're welcome to the Mill,' she said, politely ignoring the aggression in the room. 'I'm Alice Goodman, the owner's daughter and I invite you to make yourselves at home. Mikey Power, our porter, will be happy to get you sandwiches from the kitchen, and you can place your drinks orders with Mr Byrne, our barman.'

There was a derisive cheer from some of the Tans. Alice sensed, however, that the offer of hospitality had taken others by surprise, and she hoped it might divert their anger.

'Are you sure about giving them drink?' whispered Mr Byrne. 'Any more, and God knows what they'll be like!'

'Maybe,' conceded Alice. 'But I know what they'd be like if we refuse them.'

'All right,' said the barman reluctantly.

'It's the lesser of two evils, Mr Byrne. Let's do it, and hope for the best.'

Stella dropped from the wall into the back yard of the band hall. Smoke billowed up into the night sky from blown out windows on the upper story of the building, and she felt a wave of heat as she ran towards the rear door. The door was slightly ajar, and she quickly tied a handkerchief around her face, then stepped inside.

She was hit by a wave of heat and smoke, but she forced herself not to retreat. The collapsed ceiling had strewn the floor with rubble and heavy beams, and above her she could see that the fire was spreading through the top floor of the building. She picked her way carefully forward, then stopped dead. Through the swirling smoke she saw a body lying on the ground. The smoke thickened again, hiding it from view, but she had seen enough to horrify her. The body was Johnny's. Screaming in anguish, she ran towards it.

Alice realised that her plan wasn't working. She had hoped that by being hospitable the Tans might behave themselves. Instead Mikey was being loudly threatened by a constable who wasn't happy with his sandwich. Others were boisterously stamping their rifle butts on a table in the lobby and chanting for whiskey.

Alice sensed that it would take only the slightest wrong move, the most trivial imagined insult, for violence to erupt. It was time for her and the staff to make a tactical retreat, but to do that she needed to distract the Tans.

'Gentlemen! Gentlemen, if I could have your attention please,' she shouted. 'We can't serve you all quickly enough, so please, just help yourselves. A free bar with our compliments – help yourselves.'

There was a cheer from the Tans, and an exodus from the lobby towards the bar.

'Mr Byrne! Mikey!' called Alice urgently, and the two men quickly approached.

'God, the boss will have a fit about all this!' said Mr Byrne.

'Tonight I'm the boss,' said Alice. 'Better to lose a few bottles of spirits than have the place burnt down.'

'Too true!' said Mikey.

'Anyway, there's no time for that. I'm going to my room now, and I'm locking myself in. You need to do the same. The Tans will probably get drunker and drunker, so don't come out for any reason. OK?'

'Right,' said Mikey.

'Mr Byrne?'

'Yeah, right.'

'OK. Don't make it obvious, but drift away as soon as you can. And please God, we'll all come through this, and I'll see you when it's over.' Alice nodded to the two men, then she turned away and walked briskly towards her family quarters.

'Johnny!' cried Stella, 'Johnny!' She had dropped to her knees besides him, oblivious to the smoking rubble and the smouldering remains of the fallen ceiling. 'Johnny!' she cried again, shaking him. He didn't respond, and Stella felt terrified. Because of the heat, she couldn't tell if his body had gone cold. Instead she felt for a pulse, praying that she hadn't arrived too late.

She gripped his wrist. To her relief, she felt a weak beat. Using the first aid training she had received at school in Canada, she pulled aside the handkerchief she wore as a mask, put her lips to Johnny's and blew air into his mouth. Despite struggling with her own breathing because of the smoke, she breathed as quickly as she could, anxious to get as much oxygen as possible into Johnny. After about a dozen exhalations she was rewarded when he coughed, then suddenly opened his eyes.

'Stella…?' he croaked.

'Thank God!' she cried, as he coughed again, then groggily raised himself onto his elbows.

'What…what are you doing here?' he asked.

'I knew something was wrong when you didn't come back. So I came looking for you.'

'I…I can't believe you did that.'

'We're friends, Johnny. You'd do the same for me – I know you would.'

Johnny looked at her and his eyes welled with tears.

Stella squeezed his hand, then burning debris fell nearby, and she indicated the crackling flames on the storey above them. 'We need to get out of here.'

'My foot's trapped,' he said, pointing. 'I can't lift that beam.'

'Let's both try,' answered Stella. The smoke was hurting her throat and stinging her eyes, but she put her hand on the beam, and Johnny sat forward and gripped it also.

'On a count of three,' she said.

'OK.'

'One, two, three!' said Stella, then both pushed.

The beam shifted a little and Johnny tried to extract his foot.

'Push harder!' he cried.

Stella pushed with all her strength, but still Johnny couldn't free himself.

Eventually he bowed his head in defeat, and Stella watched despairingly as the fire raged ever stronger.

Alice started in fright. She had barricaded herself and Miss Hopkins inside her family quarters, and together they had pushed a heavy dresser up against the door that led to the hotel corridor. Now someone was pounding aggressively on the door.

'Open up!' shouted a man, his voice slurred. 'Open the door!'

Alice knew that barricading themselves in was a risk. But she reckoned that even if the worst came to the worst, and the Tans set fire to the Mill, she could escape out a ground floor window. There was also the risk that refusing the Tans entry might infuriate them. On balance, though, that seemed better than allowing drunken, armed men into their sanctuary.

'Open the door now!' shouted the man.

'There's only women and children in here,' cried Alice. 'Please, leave us alone, you're frightening the children.' Alice didn't know where the inspiration had come from to conjure up imaginary children. Normally she didn't like telling lies, but this wasn't a normal situation. 'Please, you're frightening them. Just take what you want and leave us.'

Alice didn't know what the Tans wanted in trying to enter her family's private quarters. Was it drunken curiosity, a desire for vandalism, a wish to loot? Whatever it was, she had to keep them at bay.

'Please,' she called out again. 'Take what you want in the hotel, but leave us women and children alone!' Alice waited, praying that they would go. Then she heard a man's voice.

'Come, on, Jock. Better pickings to be had!'

Alice heard the sound of retreating footsteps. She gave Miss Hopkins a thumbs-up sign, then sat down, her heart still thumping.

Johnny rose gingerly from the floor. His leg hurt, but he had been right about no bones being broken, and he was able to take his weight on both feet. Stella threw away the metal bar that she had found on the floor and had used as a lever to shift the beam. Johnny looked at her admiringly now, still struck by her bravery in running the gauntlet of out-of-control Tans and Auxies to rescue him from a burning building. Her clothes were as soiled and scorched as his own, but she looked triumphant now and pointed at the door.

'Time to go.'

Johnny nodded in agreement, grabbed the clarinet case, and both of them made for the door.

The upper storey was really blazing now, and Johnny kicked the back door aside, then gulped in the night air when they got outside. Stella too was drawing in lungfuls of air.

'Better not hang around for too long,' said Johnny as his breathing began to return to normal.

'Will we go over the back wall?' asked Stella.

'No, let's run around to the front. That's better for getting to the other side of town.'

'Are we not going back to the Mill?'

'Too dangerous, Stella, the area's crawling with Tans. We need to make for the outskirts of town.'

'What about Alice?'

'Alice will stay put. She'll be all right.'

'Not if the Tans burn the Mill.'

'They won't. Servicemen drink there. So they might steal drink and do some looting, but they won't burn it down.'

'Are you sure?'

'Positive.'

'OK,' said Stella. 'So what's our plan?'

'We need to get out of Balbriggan till all this dies down. When the Tans leave, we'll come back.'

'All right.'

'We still have to get away from them,' said Johnny. 'But it's shorter from here to the outskirts than going through the centre.'

'Let's go then. You lead the way.'

'Right. And whatever happens – don't stop!'

Johnny tucked the clarinet case under one arm, then began running. His leg was still a bit sore, but he rounded the corner of the burning building and sprinted out the front gate, Stella right behind him. Down a roadway to his left he saw Auxies holding prisoners at bayonet point, and to his right he heard raised voices and the sound of breaking glass.

His lungs ached from having breathed in the smoke, but he didn't slacken his speed, and he could hear Stella at his heels. He turned a corner at speed and almost collided with a Tan. The man had a case of whiskey in his arms. Johnny side-stepped him, but the man held onto the case with his left hand and grabbed Stella with his right.

'No!' she cried, trying to wriggle out of his grasp.

Johnny turned around and saw that the Tan was gripping Stella's arm. Without thinking, Johnny ran at him, all his anger at what the Tans were doing to Balbriggan crystallised in seeing his friend being mistreated.

The man saw Johnny coming and swung around, but he was too late. Johnny drove the clarinet case like a battering ram, catching the Tan squarely in the stomach. The man cried out in pain, dropping the case of whiskey. The bottles shattered on the ground, and Stella pulled herself free of his grip.

'Let's go!' cried Johnny.

Both of them ran again. They were closer to the outskirts of town here, and Johnny accelerated further on hearing a shot. He glanced behind him and saw the Tan crouched on the ground among the broken whiskey bottles. The man had drawn his revolver and now he fired twice again.

Johnny knew that it was hard to hit a moving target with a pistol, but he still felt a sense of dread. To come this close to escaping and then be hit by a stray bullet would be unbearable.

He ran flat out, Stella by his side. There were two more shots, and then they reached the edge of town and the end of the street-lights. Suddenly they were in the dark and Johnny felt his spirits soar.

'We made it, Stella! We made it!' he cried exultantly, as they ran on, deeper into the darkness and safety.

CHAPTER TWENTY-NINE

Alice looked aghast as she walked through the smoking ruins of Balbriggan. In the morning light it was clear just how much damage had been done. Pubs, shops, businesses, and dozens of houses had been destroyed. The Deeds Templar factory had been burnt down, which would mean the loss of hundreds of jobs. Even worse than the destruction was the fact that two local men, James Lawless and John Gibbons, had been killed by the Tans.

Alice wondered how Balbriggan would ever recover as she made for the train station now with Johnny and Stella. To Alice's enormous relief her friends had returned to the Mill at first light. Their clothes had been burnt and soiled, and Johnny ached in his head and leg, but they had survived. After an emotional reunion they had all swapped stories, then Johnny and Stella had bathed and changed into fresh clothes.

Alice had taken an early morning telephone call from her mother, who was now travelling home from Wexford. She had assured Mam that all was well at the Mill, with just some minor damage and theft by the Tans the previous night. Stella, too, had spoken on the telephone to her father, and Wing Commander Radcliffe was on his way from Baldonnel to Balbriggan.

Meanwhile, though, Johnny was leaving on the next train.

Alice knew she would miss him. It was tragic that two people had been killed last night, and the damage done to the town was heart breaking, but despite all that, the thing that made her saddest was the departure of her friend. Was that wrong, when people had lost their lives? Maybe it was, but she couldn't change how she felt.

She had secretly slipped the envelope with the money into his jacket pocket, and she hoped it would help him in making a fresh start in Limerick. She glanced at him now, walking between herself and Stella, all his worldly possessions in one suitcase. He looked sombre, she thought. But then the mood in the whole town was sombre, and the three friends had mostly walked in silence as they made for the station.

As they went along, the air still bitter with the smell of burnt buildings, the sun came out from behind a cloud. Alice felt its warmth upon her and she took it as a good omen. Despite the chaos of last night they had survived. And although Johnny was leaving she would see him again, she was sure of it. Feeling a bit more hopeful, she turned her face to the sun for a moment, then fell into step again with her friends as they made for the station.

Johnny waited on the platform, his feelings in turmoil. Stella and Alice had insisted on staying with him until the train came, and he sat between them. In one way it was nice to have friends seeing him off, yet in another way it prolonged the sadness of saying goodbye. There was also the sorrow he felt at what had been done to Balbriggan, but it was guiltily mixed with a sense of excitement at what the future held. Perhaps he could find out who his parents were? Perhaps he could become a musician? And meanwhile there was the thrilling prospect of working secretly for Michael Collins.

After last night he was more determined than ever to fight for independence, and to defeat the Black and Tans and Auxies. But he also knew that things were complicated, and that there were good people on the British side too, like Stella and her father. His thoughts were interrupted by the sound of an approaching train. A steam engine came puffing slowly into the station, and Johnny felt awkward now that the end had finally come.

Yet surely they would be together when all this was over. Or would they? Who could tell what might happen in the chaos of war? Stella and Alice were the two best friends he had ever had, and he felt a lump in his throat now as he rose and turned to say goodbye.

The two girls stood also, and Johnny saw that they both had tears in their eyes.

'Thanks...thanks for everything,' he said. 'You've been brilliant.'

'Good luck, Johnny,' said Alice, a tear running down her face. 'And please – please be careful.'

'I will.'

She reached out and hugged him, then turned away, dabbing her eyes with a handkerchief.

Stella looked at Johnny and tried for a smile despite her tear-filled eyes. 'Stay in touch, Johnny,' she said. 'You're...you're too good a friend to lose.'

Johnny felt his own eyes begin to well up. 'You too, Stella. You too.'

She hugged him for a moment then let him go as a porter urged passengers to board the train.

Johnny picked up his suitcase. 'Mind yourselves,' he said, a quiver in his voice.

'Safe journey,' said Stella.

'God bless, Johnny!' cried Alice as he mounted the carriage.

The train was crowded, and Johnny realised that he would be unlikely to see his friends from a window seat, so he turned back to them now. He raised his hand in farewell, and both girls waved in return. Johnny heard the porter's whistle blowing, and he gave a final wave before the doors were slammed closed. The train began to move off, and within seconds the girls were lost to view.

Johnny moved down the carriage and managed to find a seat. As the train pulled out of the station he saw the sign for Balbriggan, and he thought back over the fifteen months that he had lived in the town. Who would have thought when he left St Mary's that such adventures awaited him? That he would be recruited by Mr O'Shea, and be encouraged to be a musician by Mr Tardelli? That his two best friends would turn out to be a wealthy Balbriggan schoolgirl and the daughter of a British officer? That he would clash with Robert Foley and outwit the Tans? It had been a roller coaster ride, but now it was over, and he had to look to his new mission.

The train crossed the viaduct, picking up speed as it left Balbriggan. Johnny watched the town recede, then he slowly turned away, ready for whatever came next, and eager to play his part.

EPILOGUE

Wing Commander Radcliffe left the RAF when the War of Independence ended. He returned to Canada where he worked in the timber industry. Stella went to university in Montreal, and qualified as a child psychologist, eventually working in the Bloor Clinic, where she had once been treated herself.

Mrs Goodman ran the Mill Hotel for many years. Alice married and had children, and she and her husband modernised and ran the renamed North Coast Hotel and Restaurant, after Mrs Goodman retired.

Mr O'Shea escaped from jail and fought with the rebels for the rest of the war. He went on to become a senior civil servant in the new Irish government.

Mr Tardelli continued to teach music in Alice's old school, while his town band grew ever more successful and went on to win many prizes over the years.

Robert broke his leg in a school match and had to give up playing rugby. He followed in his father's footsteps and became a surgeon, then emigrated to Australia.

Johnny remained active in the fight for independence. He joined the Army School of Music in the newly-formed Irish Free State, and fulfilled his dream of being a professional musician, becoming a leading player in the Army Number One Band. He stayed in touch with Stella and Alice and whenever Stella visited Ireland the three friends got together. Their lives had gone in very different directions, but their old rapport remained, as they shared their memories of 1920, a year that none of them would ever forget.

HISTORICAL NOTE

The War of Independence began in June 1919 and ended with the truce of July 1921. This was followed by negotiations in London, and in December 1921 a treaty with Britain was signed. The treaty was ratified by Dáil Eireann in January 1922, which resulted in the founding of the Irish Free State.

British troops began to leave Ireland in January 1922, and Michael Collins, the Irish Commander-in-Chief, took possession of Dublin Castle from Lord Lieutenant FitzAlan.

The Royal Irish Constabulary was disbanded, to be replaced by a new, unarmed police force, the Garda Síochána.

The Black and Tans left Ireland as part of the British withdrawal, and the camp at Gormanston was the base from which the last group departed.

Gormanston Camp remained a military installation with the founding of the Irish Free State. It served as a centre for refugees from Northern Ireland during the early days of the Troubles, and today is still the property of the Department of Defence, serving as a reserve airstrip.

Johnny, Stella, Alice and their families are fictitious, as is the Mill Hotel. The historical events described are real, however, and the assassination bid on Lord French, the replacement of the RAF by the Black and Tans at Gormanston, and the burning of Balbriggan were all actual events.

The sack of Balbriggan, as it became known, caused an outrage that was reported upon internationally, and that lead to questions being asked in the Houses of Parliament. Two civilians, James Lawless, and John Gibbons, were killed, forty-five homes were damaged or destroyed, shops and pubs were burnt down and the Deeds Templar hosiery factory, a major employer, was also destroyed.

Balbriggan was eventually rebuilt and is considerably bigger today than in 1920. Much has changed, but the library, the train station, the railway viaduct and the Martello tower can still be seen.

Brian Gallagher, Dublin 2017